Days of Small Adventures

Tales of unforgettable experiences, first loves, and anxious journeys

L.J. Perkins

Copyright © 2025 L.J. Perkins

All rights reserved. No portion of this book may be reproduced in any form without prior permission from the copyright owner of this book. For permissions contact: ljpstories@outlook.com

ISBN: 9798272677358

DEDICATION

I dedicate this book to my ever-supportive family and friends, who cheer me on in every pursuit, and to the friends—real and remembered—who slip between the lines of these stories. And, of course, to Dexter, my cocker-spaniel and writing sidekick, for his un-wavering company.

CONTENTS

PREFACE vii

INTRODUCTION ix

THE YEARS WE BURNED BRIGHT 1

    Chapter One: **Eighties Child** 3

    Chapter Two: **The Next Chapter** 13

    Chapter Three: **The One and Only** 21

    Chapter Four: **Chasing Stars** 27

    Chapter Five: **Lights, Camera, Action** 35

THE CROOKED PATH TO LOVE 47

    Chapter One: **Young Love** 49

    Chapter Two: **Growing Up** 53

    Chapter Three: **Broadening Horizons** 57

    Chapter Four: **Road to Heartbreak** 67

    Chapter Five: **Irresistible** 77

    Chapter Six: "**The One**" 89

MARRAKECH 101

    Chapter One: **Travel Apprehensions** 103

    Chapter Two: **Unfamiliar Territory** 107

    Chapter Three: **Into the Unknown** 113

    Chapter Four: **Shell-Shocked** 119

    Chapter Five: **Breaking Boundaries** 123

ABOUT THE AUTHOR 129

PREFACE

Every life holds stories worth telling. I've always been fascinated by other people's experiences and inspired to turn my own memories into tales for others to enjoy.

Writing has been a lifelong passion, from music and stories to keeping diaries. Rediscovering journals spanning more than thirty years sparked this collection, where my experiences take shape on the page.

Following the release of my first book, *Against All Odds*, I'm delighted to share this second collection. These three short stories capture life's adventures—the fun, mischief, and reflections of growing up; the twists and turns of finding a lifelong partner; and the thrill of discovering new cultures and overcoming travel fears.

Through these stories, you'll find moments of laughter, wonder, and insight—a celebration of life's richness and the lessons it offers.

INTRODUCTION

This book is a collection of three short stories, which have been compiled into one story book. The sections are listed below.

The Years we Burned Bright chronicles Lisa's school life and social adventures, capturing the joys, challenges, and friendships that shaped her coming-of-age during the 1980s and 1990s.

The Crooked Path to Love traces Charlotte's journey from childhood to adulthood, exploring the many twists and turns of love—mostly unrequited—until she finally discovers "the one".

Marrakech follows Louisa as she navigates uncharted territory during a politically turbulent time, revealing how embracing the journey led to unexpected and transformative experiences.

THE YEARS WE BURNED BRIGHT

CHAPTER ONE
EIGHTIES CHILD

Highly Commended: the words stared back at me from the examination slip. Not failure, but not quite success either.

"Don't be too upset. That's still a really good result," my mum said gently, offering an encouraging smile.

"I really tried this time. What do I have to do to get a Distinction? Vicki always manages it..." I sighed, sinking onto a worn wooden stump outside the dance studio.

Saturday mornings were usually my favourite time of the week. I loved attending dance classes with Vicki—my best friend since we were three—but no matter how much I practiced, I couldn't seem to shake the nerves that came with exams. Vicki, on the other hand, danced through them with the effortless confidence I envied. We were a couple of years into Acrobatics and Modern dance, and while I adored it, falling short of a Distinction again had me questioning whether I'd ever be good enough to fulfil my dreams of becoming a dancer.

"Don't be sad," came a familiar voice. Vicki stepped out of the studio, spotting me on the tree stump looking clearly deflated. "Tell you what, I'll show you some of my tricks. Maybe next time you'll get that Distinction! And tonight, when you come over for the sleepover, we'll have a disco and go over the new routines."

I couldn't help but smile. Vicki always knew how to lift my spirits. We were complete opposites in many ways—me, the reserved one; her, the bold spark. Somehow, it worked. We were like sisters more than friends.

Her confidence had always inspired me. I followed her lead, whether we were dancing in front of classmates or performing at school assemblies. Her competitive streak even rubbed off on me from time to time.

"Hey Vicki, which Maths book are you on now?" I asked one morning during school.

"The Owl book," she replied, grinning. "Almost finished it, too."

Our Maths lessons were self-paced, and each student was provided with a series of colourful *Hey Mathematics* books to work through. Somehow, progressing to the next book felt like a major achievement.

"Oh... I thought we were on the same one," I said, trying to hide my surprise.

"We were," she said casually, "but I took mine home and completed some extra pages over the weekend, so the teacher gave me the next one up."

A surge of competitiveness lit up inside me. That evening, I took my book home and powered through as many exercises as I could, determined to catch up. And I did—briefly. Vicki always seemed to be one step ahead though, flaunting the next shiny book while I was still playing catch-up. I didn't even like Maths that much!

That same feeling of competition kicked in again one afternoon when I came home from school and realised my favourite book—*The Naughtiest Girl in the School* by Enid Blyton—was missing.

Oh no! I thought. I'd been looking forward to reading it before bed.

The next morning, as we walked into class, Vicki called out, "Hey, Lisa, you left this behind yesterday."

"My book! Thanks for finding it," I said, relieved.

"It's a brilliant story, isn't it?" she added, smiling as she handed it back.

"You read it?" I asked, wide-eyed.

"Yeah, hope you don't mind—it looked interesting. You know me—bookworm through and through. I think I'll get the next one from the library."

I was fuming. I was only halfway through, and now she'd not only read the whole thing, but she was already planning to get ahead in the series. I threw myself into a reading frenzy that week, desperate to keep pace. It was exhausting being competitive.

My friendship with Vicki had all the dynamics of a sibling relationship—one moment we were laughing and dancing together, the next we were in competition with one another.

Of course, we got up to mischief now and then too—what childhood friendship didn't come with a touch of rebellion?

One memorable episode involved a rather misguided attempt to assert our superiority over our self-proclaimed archenemies: the kids from St. Anne's School.

There was no real reason for the animosity between us Thameside students and the St. Anne's crowd. It was just an unspoken rule that we didn't mix. If we happened to cross paths after school, it was customary to exchange scowls, as if we'd inherited a feud no one could properly explain.

I'll never forget the day that underlying tension boiled to the surface. It was an otherwise ordinary Tuesday afternoon. Vicki and I were playing in the local park after school when she spotted a girl from St. Anne's loitering nearby.

"There's that St. Anne's girl again," Vicki sneered, narrowing her eyes. "She keeps staring at us. I can't stand her—I'm going to give her a piece of my mind."

Without another word, she marched over, exchanged a few quick words with the girl, then came running back to me, grinning like she'd just won a prize.

"I don't think she'll be back here tomorrow," she said smugly. "I just told her exactly what I think of her and her St. Anne's crew."

From across the park, I then spotted the same girl speaking with an adult—clearly her mother. They both looked over in our direction. Vicki was still riding the high of her little confrontation, but I suddenly felt a knot of unease twist in my stomach.

"Um... Vicki... looks like she just told that woman what happened, and I think she's coming over here. That must be her mum."

I braced myself for witnessing an awkward exchange—perhaps a telling-off or an uncomfortable scolding. But what happened next left me completely stunned.

The woman marched right past Vicki without a glance, came straight up to me, and—without uttering a single word—struck me across the face with such force that it nearly knocked me off my feet. I staggered, stunned, trying to comprehend what had just happened.

"Oh my god, are you alright?" Vicki gasped, suddenly serious.

"She hit me," I said, voice trembling with shock and fury. "That woman just hit me—and I didn't even do anything. That slap wasn't meant for me... was it?"

My cheek burned with the sting of injustice, but more than that, I was left reeling by the sheer unfairness of it all.

We left the park without a word; the silence between us said everything. The walk home felt unusually long. Vicki's guilt was palpable—she knew I had taken the punishment meant for her—and I, for my part, was adrift with a mixture of embarrassment and disbelief.

It wasn't a memory I cherished, but there were plenty that I did: roller-skating in the park, sleepovers complete with midnight feasts, spontaneous visits to photo booths where we pulled silly faces, trips to the local lido, and countless other carefree moments. School non-uniform days were another highlight. Vicki and I would plan our outfits in advance, investing far more thought into them than we did into our schoolwork.

"Mum, these are the boots I was telling you about," I said one afternoon as she walked into the lounge to find I'd paused a video of Madonna mid-performance.

She raised an eyebrow. "Hmm, not sure you need something with heels that high, but let's go into town on Saturday and see if we can find something more suitable."

That Saturday, we headed to the local department store. While my mum browsed the shelves for practical, sensible options, I gravitated toward rows of shiny white stilettos. I tried on several pairs, struggling to balance as I attempted to strut up and down the aisles. A few older women glanced my way disapprovingly.

In the end, we struck a compromise: a pair of modest kitten heels—grown-up enough to feel special, but still age-appropriate in my mum's eyes.

When non-uniform day finally arrived, I couldn't wait to wear my new heels to school. As I made my way along the veranda outside the classrooms, I spotted Vicki running toward me. She was wearing a pair of bright pink high heels.

Seriously? I thought. How come she gets to wear proper heels and I don't?

One place I knew Vicki's high-heeled shoes wouldn't be making an appearance, however, was on our Brownie pack holiday. I was both excited and nervous about our upcoming trip to Somerset. It would be my first time away from home without my parents, and I wondered if homesickness might catch me off guard.

"What are you bringing for your dessert?" Vicki asked one day as we chatted about the trip. "I'm taking some cookies."

I loved the idea that we'd each bring a dessert from home to enjoy after dinner each night—it somehow made the thought of being away feel a little less daunting.

"Definitely my mum's homemade jam tarts," I replied with a grin. "I could eat a hundred of them!"

Before long, the summer holidays arrived, and the day of our trip rolled around.

"Have a lovely time, won't you?" my mum said warmly, as she and my dad hugged me tightly.

"I will! I'll write to you," I called, waving from the coach as we set off on our adventure—many of us leaving our families for the very first time.

After a couple of hours on the road and a brief toilet stop, we arrived at our accommodation, which looked like a giant wooden hut from the outside and resembled a school hall within. As we chose our camp beds and began unpacking, we were then approached and told to take our Tupperware and treat tins straight to the kitchen.

That evening, we were seated at round tables scattered around the hall for dinner. I ate most of the shepherd's pie served to me, saving room for what I hoped would be at least two of my mum's famous jam tarts.

As Brown Owl and her team began distributing the desserts, I scanned the trays anxiously but couldn't spot my mum's jam tarts anywhere. Then, to my horror, a slice of apple pie was placed in front of me. I looked up, waiting for someone to realise the mix-up, but Brown Owl moved on without a second glance.

"Why aren't we getting our own treats?" I whispered to Vicki.

"Oh, I think they're sharing them all out," she replied casually.

A huge wave of disappointment swept over me—I hated apple pie. And then, to make matters worse, I spotted one of my mum's jam tarts sitting on another Brownie's plate, about to be eaten. I was outraged!

I managed to hide my annoyance for the rest of the week, despite only receiving one of my mum's jam tarts during the entire trip. On the bright side, I did earn my entertainment badge that week for performing a successful stand-up comedy routine!

To make up for the jam tart injustice, Vicki and I treated ourselves to a trip to our local bakery once we were home. That's where she introduced me to split-finger doughnuts—my new favourite sweet treat.

The bakery quickly became my favourite destination. I remember, on one particular day, deciding to go there alone.

As I stood before the glass cabinet, surveying the dazzling selection of sugary delights, I suddenly felt myself rising—quite literally. In an instant, I was lifted off the ground, held high above the counter, peering down at the cakes from above.

"Give her whatever she wants!" boomed a male voice beside my ear.

The man was a stranger, a customer who had entered the bakery just moments before. He had hoisted me up and offered to pay for whatever cakes I desired. In hindsight, it was probably inappropriate, but this was the 1980s, and I was a child who adored cake!

"I'll have two split-finger doughnuts, a lemon curd doughnut, a jam doughnut, and two iced buns, please!" I speedily announced, determined to place my order before the generous stranger had a chance to change his mind.

The shop assistant smiled, filled my request, and handed me a box. I expressed my gratitude to both her and the man, then happily made my way home.

The following week, I returned at the same time, hoping lightning might strike twice.

But this visit unfolded very differently.

As I stepped inside, I was startled to see a middle-aged man collapsed on the floor, his body slumped against the wall behind the queue. He was unconscious but breathing. Something that looked like chewing gum was lodged in his mouth and appeared to be stuck to the wall. The scene was unsettling. Yet, remarkably, the bakery continued operating as if nothing unusual had occurred. Customers stepped around him, calmly purchasing their loaves and pastries while the man lay there, unmoving.

Could that be the same man who had lifted me up the week before? I wondered.

"Can I help you?" the woman behind the counter asked, pulling me from my thoughts.

"Yes... just one split-finger doughnut, please," I replied quietly.

I paid, took my cake, and walked past the man still lying on the floor. Surely someone had called an ambulance by now, I reassured myself. Still, the image lingered with me for years.

CHAPTER TWO
THE NEXT CHAPTER

Looking back on my childhood, I realised it had been filled with moments of triumph, mischief, and discovery—little adventures that shaped who I was becoming. Vicki had been at the heart of many of those memories, from our dance classes to sleepovers and park escapades. But after she moved to the other side of town and transferred to a new school, I had to learn how to navigate life without my closest companion by my side.

Thankfully, I had always been friendly with Joanna—a like-minded girl who, coincidentally, was also navigating the loss of her best friend to a school move.

Joanna and I shared a special connection. We were born just a day apart, in the same hospital, so our families had known each other even before we really knew ourselves.

We both had a passion for creativity—music, singing, acting, and art were constant threads in our conversations and play. I was especially envious of Joanna learning to play the violin. I longed to be the one carrying an important-looking instrument case to and from school each week. Instead, I made do with the recorder. I gave it my all, of course, but it was hard to feel like a proper musician when your instrument fit into your coat pocket.

In our final year of primary school, Joanna and I made countless memories together. Her house was on my walk home from school, and I'd often stop by on my way back. Some days, I stayed for tea. Over dishes like salmon plait or chicken cacciatore, we'd chat and unwind from the school day, usually with a Madonna album playing in the background.

Being creative souls, we often bounced ideas off each other—usually the imaginative kind. One day, after watching a heartfelt appeal for donations to help starving children in Africa, we found ourselves feeling unexpectedly entrepreneurial.

"It makes sense, we both love knitting, so why not knit some dolls and sell them at school break time?" Joanna suggested.

"Yes, that sounds fun. And doing it for charity might help get people's attention, don't you think?" I replied.

"Exactly—if we give the money to Oxfam, people will be more likely to support us. Plus, it'll feel good to do a good deed."

With the teachers' permission and several hours of work knitting behind us, we began selling our knitted dolls at school break times. We positioned a school desk at the end of the veranda outside the upper-school classrooms and began selling.

A few curious people turned into a much bigger crowd, and after the first sale came the next—and the next.

"Have you got any knitted animals?" came one pupil's enquiry. "Can you make a doll that looks like me?" asked another.

Before we knew it, we were spending every evening knitting more and more stock to sell; I even roped in my mum to help with the mass production. Every day at morning break, we would be in the same spot, selling countless dolls and watching our profits grow and grow. We were loving it!

"Hey Joanna—what are they doing over there?" I asked one Monday morning break time, pointing at three other girls in our class.

"It looks like they're setting up a stall to sell some things too," replied Joanna.

On a quick inspection, we quickly realised that they had not only taken our idea but were executing it more effectively. Their products were more colourful, and they had a larger team actively producing stock.

"They can't do that! That was our idea," I exclaimed.

"There's not much we can do about it," Joanna replied with a shrug. "Maybe we should just shut up shop and hand the profits we've made so far over to Oxfam."

I nodded, reluctantly agreeing. But on our way home from school, our attention drifted elsewhere.

"You know," Joanna said suddenly, "I'd absolutely love a quarter of honeycombs right now."

"Mmm, me too. It's so unfair we have to walk past a sweet shop every day," I sighed. "I don't even get my pocket money until Friday."

We exchanged a look.

"Are you thinking what I'm thinking?" I asked.

"We can't," Joanna said firmly. "We already agreed the money was for charity."

"I know... but we worked hard. Don't we deserve a little treat?"

Before we knew it, we were both striding toward the sweet shop and placing our orders. I felt a pang of guilt—but the honeycombs were absolutely worth it!

The end of primary school marked a time of significant change, not least because Joanna and I were heading to different secondary schools that September—meaning I'd once again have to navigate the challenge of building new friendships.

Fortunately, Donna—a friend since nursery and primary school—was starting at the same secondary school as me. Our parents had arranged shared lifts to and from school, which made the transition a little easier.

It was comforting to begin this new chapter alongside a familiar face, and Donna and I soon began spending more time together outside of school too. She lived on a quiet street, and we would often spend long summer evenings playing tennis there, stepping aside whenever a car came by. Occasionally, her neighbours would join in, adding to the sense of community.

Donna, being naturally sociable, quickly found her place among new friends at school. Not long after, I found a kindred spirit of my own—Claire. We bonded instantly over our shared love for Madonna, and a new friendship blossomed.

Claire lived close to school and often invited me to her house for lunch. Our routine quickly became familiar: we'd eat while watching *Neighbours* on TV, then wander down to the local garage to buy sweets or ice pops to enjoy on the walk back.

One lunchtime, Claire shared some exciting news.

"Hey Lisa, my mum said there's a new toy store opening in town soon—and guess what? Philip Schofield is going to be there to cut the ribbon! We should go and get his autograph!"

"Oh wow! Someone famous in our hometown? That's so exciting—yes, let's go meet him" I said, already picturing the moment.

A few weeks later, we found ourselves outside the newly refurbished toy store. Though we'd mostly outgrown toys, there was still a thrill in seeing someone from television in real life.

The queue stretched from the entrance, through the aisles, and up to the second floor. Eventually, we caught sight of him.

"He's smaller than I imagined," Claire observed.

"Yeah, isn't it strange?" I replied.

As we reached the front, he smiled. "Hi, what's your name?"

"Lisa," I said, returning the smile. He signed a glossy photo card and handed it to me.

After Claire got hers, we posed for a quick photo for the local newspaper. Then, giggling, we slipped out.

"Wasn't he lovely?" Claire said as we descended the stairs.

"Yeah. Hey... do you think he's parked out front?" I asked.

"Probably not. There's a car park out the back," she replied.

We ran around to the rear and caught a glimpse of him getting into his car. Claire grinned. "Let's write down his number plate!"

We waved as he drove away, feeling smug and slightly giddy at having seen him up close, away from the crowds.

A few months later, Claire had more news—though this time, it wasn't so thrilling.

"I've got something to tell you, Lisa," she said, her voice hesitant.

"Go on then—what is it? Don't tell me another celebrity's coming to town," I joked, trying to lighten the moment.

"Not quite," she replied, lowering her eyes. "My dad's job is relocating... and we're moving."

"Oh? Where to?" I asked casually.

"Guildford," she said.

"Guildford? That's miles away," I said, the worry creeping into my voice. "So, you're changing schools too?"

Claire nodded. She looked down, uncertain. I could see she'd been dreading telling me. I was upset too—once again, I felt the loss of someone I had grown close to, someone who understood the little thrills of my world.

We made the most of the time we had left, and after she moved, her dad kindly brought me over to visit. It was lovely to see her again, to explore her new house, and hear how she was settling in. But for me, moving on would take a little longer. After all, who else was I going to stalk celebrities with?

CHAPTER THREE
THE ONE AND ONLY

After Claire moved away, I found myself drifting between social circles, unsure of where I belonged. I often felt like an outsider—watching from the edges rather than joining in.

One afternoon, while waiting for a Maths lesson to begin, a girl named Michelle approached my desk.

"Hi, is anyone sitting here?" she asked, pointing to the empty chair beside me.

"No, go ahead," I replied with a smile.

I'd seen Michelle many times before, but we'd never spoken. I was quietly pleased she'd chosen to sit next to me; sometimes the class's self-proclaimed queen bee, Julie, would plonk herself beside me and be obnoxious the entire lesson.

From that day on, Michelle always chose the seat beside mine, and before long, we became lunchtime buddies too. There was something reassuring about her calm, grounded energy. Like me, she didn't crave the spotlight, and we connected easily—bonding over shared experiences, including our mutual efforts to avoid difficult classmates like Julie, whom we jokingly nicknamed "Football Face" for her notably large, round head.

One lunchtime, while reminiscing about my friendship with Claire and our memorable encounter with Philip Schofield, the topic of celebrities—and specifically our current favourite popstars—came up.

"You know Chesney Hawkes lives in Berkshire, right?" Michelle said casually, biting into her sandwich.

"What, really? Are you sure? How do you know that?" I asked, suddenly alert.

"It's in *Smash Hits* magazine this week. It says he lives in Sunningdale. He mentioned it on TV-am too, I think."

"That's not far away at all! We could easily get the train there," I said, a plan already forming.

Michelle laughed. "Let's go this weekend! I'll ask Sushma to come too—between the three of us, we could probably track down where he lives!"

That Saturday, armed with train tickets and teenage enthusiasm, we set off on our unofficial celebrity stakeout. The slow train carried us to Sunningdale, where we disembarked with no real plan, just hope.

"Which way should we head?" Michelle asked.

"I didn't realise it would be this big," I replied, scanning the unfamiliar streets.

We noticed a steady stream of people heading in one direction and decided to follow them, hoping for a sign. Eventually, the crowd thinned, and we found ourselves at a quiet residential junction.

"How about this road?" Sushma suggested, pointing up a leafy street.

"Why not?" Michelle agreed. "It's not like we have a better plan."

"Would it be weird to ask someone where he lives?" I asked, half-joking.

Michelle grinned. "Definitely a little weird. But maybe worth it. And since it was your idea... you can ask that man walking toward us."

It was a little embarrassing, but I mustered up the courage.

"Excuse me—do you happen to know where Chesney Hawkes lives?" I asked the man, doing my best to mask the embarrassment in my voice.

"Sorry, no," he replied, continuing on his way.

"Well, that was awkward," I grimaced. "Someone else can ask the next person."

Over the next ten minutes, we took turns approaching people along the quiet street, but most either hadn't heard of Chesney or simply shook their heads. We were close to giving up when we decided to pop into a corner shop across the road for a drink.

As we browsed, a group of girls around our age burst in, chatting and laughing with the kind of energy that caught our attention.

"I wonder if they're looking for his house too?" Sushma whispered.

"Let's follow them," Michelle said, without hesitation.

We trailed behind as they left the shop and turned into a private, tree-lined road with enormous houses. About a hundred metres in, they stopped outside a home with towering iron gates and sat down casually, as though it were a familiar routine.

"This must be it!" I gasped, barely able to contain my excitement.

"I think we've struck gold," Michelle beamed. "Look—the electric gates are opening!"

A brand-new white Ford Fiesta pulled out of the drive. The driver paused to chat briefly with the girls before giving us a friendly wave and driving off.

"I think that was Chesney's brother!" I squealed.

Sushma went over to speak with the other girls and returned with an update. "They said Chesney's in America right now—but he'll be back next week."

We exchanged triumphant smiles. Our celebrity-spotting mission had paid off.

In the weeks that followed, we made regular weekend trips to Sunningdale, joining the growing crowd of fans who gathered outside his home. Our persistence paid off—not only did we meet Chesney himself, but also his brother, mum, dad, a few of his bandmates, and even some of his celebrity friends.

The family often opened their gates and welcomed fans into the front garden to chat, take photos, and collect autographs. We were in our element, burning through rolls of camera film and living out every teenage dream. On weekdays, we proudly brought our photos to school, drawing crowds around our desks as we relived our encounters—wide-eyed and full of stories.

"I heard they're planning to stop fans from visiting—apparently the neighbours have had enough," announced Julie.

"Why's Football Face getting involved?" Michelle whispered.

"I heard a crazed fan actually crawled through their cat flap while they were out and took a bunch of photos in Chesney's bedroom—then had the nerve to ask him to sign them afterwards!" added another classmate.

"Wow... we're not that extreme," I muttered.

"No, definitely not," Michelle replied. "We're just having a bit of fun—nothing invasive."

"Maybe if you spent less time chasing Z-listers and more time revising like the rest of us, you'd have a shot at passing your exams. Keep this up, and you'll both end up flipping burgers for a living!" Julie sneered, striding off.

Michelle and I shared a glance of pure disdain.

As it happened, Chesney's neighbours wouldn't have to endure the commotion for much longer. Within a few months, the excitement had fizzled out, but true to form, our next adventure wasn't far away.

CHAPTER FOUR
CHASING STARS

Meeting new friends always brought a spark of excitement—especially when it came with the bonus of being drawn into their wider circle. Michelle had recently become friends with a girl named Lynn, who was connected to her through a tangle of sibling friendships. Although Lynn was a little older, we quickly hit it off and soon found ourselves spending weekends together at one another's homes.

Lynn introduced us to a new musical obsession—The Osmond Boys, sons of the original Osmonds. We were instantly captivated, often spending entire evenings listening to their music and chatting endlessly about them.

"I heard they're coming to London soon for a few shows—maybe we could try to meet them?" Lynn proposed one night.

"I'd be up for that!" Michelle replied enthusiastically.

I was just as eager. Michelle and I had recently discovered the magic of her mum's National Rail card, which allowed us to buy child tickets for just £1 each. It had become our gateway to London—and any excuse to visit the city was good enough for me.

We spent the next few weeks planning our next celebrity stakeout. Lynn had joined a fan club, which gave the dates of the Osmonds' trip and the hotel they would be staying in.

The day of our celebrity hunt finally arrived. We jumped on the fast train to London, dressed in our carefully selected outfits with cameras and pen and paper at the ready.

We headed straight to the Langham Hilton Hotel in the West End. We could see other girls our age huddled outside the hotel and began chatting to them. No one seemed to be leaving the hotel, so we hung around chatting with the new girls.

A little later, I noticed a white van outside the hotel with the back doors open. Some men were carrying large items and placing them in the back. One item looked like a platinum disc award that a band would receive for notable record sales, but there were no signs of the Osmond Boys.

"I hope they come out soon—I'm starting to feel hungry," I said.

"Yeah—me too. It's pretty boring just waiting around," Lynn replied.

Just then, a man came walking over toward us and made a beeline for me.

"Hi," he said with a smile. "Who are you waiting for?"

He had a kind of Australian accent. He was obviously a guest at the hotel and curious as to why some crowds had gathered.

"The Osmond Boys," I replied.

"Oh wow—that's impressive," he responded with a smile before walking away and getting into the white van we had seen earlier.

"Look! Over there!" Michelle suddenly piped up. "That's them coming out of the hotel!"

We experienced a surge of excitement and hurried over to the entrance steps to the hotel along with all the other girls who were waiting.

A mad frenzy of camera flashes and calls to get each boy's attention unfolded.

"Nathan! Nathan! Over here!" shouted one girl.

"David—here—can I have my picture taken with you?" requested another.

The boys soon became detached from each other, with several girls surrounding each one. Their parents and security staff tried to stay close and ensure they were not being overwhelmed.

They politely signed autographs and posed for pictures, then began walking away from the hotel and towards a very busy Oxford Street. We followed them through shopping centres, into clothing shops, and finally into a fast-food restaurant. Hordes of girls surrounded them as they tried to quietly eat their food in peace.

From there, they headed into a record store. We followed, keeping a respectful distance so as not to crowd them.

"Hey, Lisa! Look at this," Michelle said, picking up a record. "Isn't this what we saw earlier?"

"Oh wow, yes! That's the disc those guys were loading into the van."

"It's Crowded House!" Michelle squealed. "Do you recognise anyone on the cover?"

"Yes—the guy in the middle! He's the one who asked who we were waiting for outside the hotel. I can't believe a pop star came over and spoke to me, and I had no idea who he was!"

"He must've been a bit put out that you weren't waiting for him," said Shelley, a girl from London who had joined us for our Osmonds-themed trawl around the city.

Shelley lived in Streatham Hill—a part of London we'd never been to before. That afternoon, when the Osmond Boys had returned to their hotel, we accompanied Shelley back to her part of town; we had free travel all over London, after all, and it would be silly to waste that.

En route to Shelley's house, we found ourselves in Brixton.

"Wow—this place is really buzzing with energy," I noticed.

"Yeah—it's cool. Look! There's 'Electric Avenue'," spotted Michelle before we all broke into the famous Eddie Grant song.

Shelley led us to her house, welcomed us in, and made us all a drink.

"So, you seem to know a lot about the Osmonds," said Lynn.

"Yeah—I've been following them for a while, and I know that when they're in London there's a particular Mormon church they attend, so I've been going there regularly and finding out more about them."

"Gosh—you've really gone to an effort to be in their world!" replied Lynn.

"I really have. In fact, I'm going next Sunday to the church to be baptised officially into the Mormon religion," Shelley informed us.

We all looked at each other in shock.

"Really?" I asked. "That's quite a commitment!"

"I know, but I've thought it through, and it feels right. Why don't you guys all come along to watch next Sunday?" she suggested.

It struck me how far our obsession with pop idols had taken us already—and now it seemed to be leading us somewhere even stranger.

We all smiled and nodded—another chance to go to London was definitely appealing, and there might be a chance to see the Osmond Boys in the church.

The next week seemed to drag—we couldn't take our minds off the upcoming experience of heading to London to a famous Mormon church and seeing our new-found friend be baptised.

When the day finally arrived, we dressed in our Sunday best and boarded the train to London, then had a short tube journey to South Kensington.

Entering the church felt daunting. It was far larger than expected, already bustling with people.

"I feel a bit out of place," Michelle whispered.

"Me too—I feel like everyone is looking at us," I admitted.

"It's just that they don't know us," Lynn reassured. "Shelley did say that they were all very friendly and welcoming here."

Just then, a friendly face came bounding over.

"You made it! I'm so pleased you're here!" beamed Shelley.

"We wouldn't miss it!" replied Lynn.

"Although we're *really* here to see if the Osmond Boys show up," Michelle jokingly whispered in my ear.

We followed Shelley inside, taking our seats and joining in awkwardly with hymns we didn't know. I found myself glancing around, half-hoping for a familiar face.

"Doesn't look like they're coming," I murmured.

"Probably busy," Lynn said with a shrug.

"Look—there's Shelley," Michelle whispered.

She was dressed in a plain white jumpsuit.

I blinked. "What on earth is she wearing?"

"It's the baptism jumpsuit," Lynn explained. "She told me they have to wear it in the tank."

"She's going in a tank?" My voice was a little too loud.

"Sshh!" Lynn whispered. "We're trying to blend in! I mean the baptism font thingy."

After a few moments, the baptism began. For a while, we sat in silence, watching with curiosity as our friend underwent the cleansing ritual. As a few words were spoken by a church member, we remained composed, though still curious. But something about the solemn atmosphere, the unusual outfit Shelley wore, and the expectation that we remain serious all at once set us off. Michelle's shoulders began to shake, then mine. The harder we tried to stop, the worse it got, until the three of us were quietly convulsing with laughter, drawing sharp glances from the pews around us.

"Oi, you two—stop it!" Lynn hissed. Even she soon gave in, and the three of us were quietly shaking with giggles. The harder we tried to suppress them, the louder they became, drawing disapproving glances from those around us. By the time the service ended, I could hardly meet anyone's eyes and couldn't wait to escape.

Still, we couldn't leave without speaking to Shelley. We offered our congratulations, then quickly slipped away.

On the train home, Michelle sighed. "I don't know how we didn't get thrown out of there."

"Me neither—not sure what it was that set us off," I said, replaying the memory.

"It wasn't really that funny—we just caught the giggles," added Lynn.

Thankfully, Shelley never found out we'd laughed all the way through her baptism—but after that day, we never saw her or the Osmond Boys again. Michelle and I, however, stayed inseparable, always on the lookout for our next big thrill.

CHAPTER FIVE
LIGHTS, CAMERA, ACTION

By our mid-teens, Michelle and I had become experts at squeezing as much fun as possible out of our free time. Whether we were chasing after pop stars, braving rollercoasters at theme parks, or borrowing her mum's video camera to film our own ridiculous sketches, we never let a weekend pass quietly. Michelle even managed to land herself a role in a magazine photo story—an appearance that caused quite the stir at school once it was in print.

Our next joint adventure came when we discovered Michelle's mum had a knack for getting hold of audience tickets to popular TV shows.

"My mum's just got some tickets for *Blind Date*. Want to come?" Michelle asked one morning at school.

"Er... yes, please! Do you think we'll actually get on TV?" I replied, my voice bright with anticipation.

"Ha! You never know," she grinned.

A few friends joined us, and before long, we were on the train to London's South Bank, heading for LWT Studios. Sitting in the audience was surreal—watching the cameras swing into place, the presenters getting prepped, and the whole buzz of TV magic unfolding just metres away. There was a bit of waiting around, but it didn't matter. We were hooked.

When the episode finally aired, we scanned the screen desperately for a glimpse of ourselves, but to our disappointment, we didn't appear once. Still, that didn't dampen our enthusiasm. More tickets soon followed, and we found ourselves at recordings of shows like *Men Behaving Badly* and *The Crystal Rose Show*.

One evening, the phone rang.

"Lisa! You'll never guess what Mum's managed to get us this time," Michelle burst out.

"Ooh, which show?" I asked, bracing myself.

"*Top of the Pops*!" she shrieked.

I nearly dropped the phone. This wasn't just another chance to be seen on TV—it meant live music, big-name bands, and the sheer thrill of being part of something iconic. I could hardly contain myself.

Needless to say, word spread fast amongst our friends—everyone wanted in.

Within a couple of weeks, we were off to London—our second home—once again!

"Which bands are playing tonight?" asked our friend, Saby, as the train pulled out of the station.

"We're seeing The Stereo MCs, Crowded House, Dr Alban, and a few others," replied Michelle.

"Amazing! This is going to be so much fun!" Saby smiled.

When we arrived at Elstree Studios, the staff ushered us into a holding room and gave us instructions. This was different from any other TV show we'd seen recorded—we wouldn't be seated; instead, we would be moving around the studio floor between stages.

"Let's try to stick together," Michelle suggested, "but we need to be ready for when a song is finishing so we can rush to the next stage and get to the front. We want to do our best to get on TV this time!"

After a short wait, we were allowed into the main studio area.

"Wow, it's quite small in here—looks so much bigger on TV," I remarked as we walked through the studio.

Once the studio filled up with audience members and the doors closed, the first band appeared on one of the stages and began setting up.

"Quick! Let's go over there—it looks like this is the first stage!" Michelle urged.

"Who are these guys?" asked Lynn.

"Stereo MCs," Michelle and I said in unison.

Within minutes, the audience was hushed as instructions came over the loudspeaker: "Quiet on set... Places... Stand by."

My friends and I exchanged excited glances, then...

"Action!" shouted the director.

We were too busy focusing on the band to notice a presenter, lit on a podium across the studio, speaking into a camera to introduce the show. The cameras then swung around onto the stage, and the band started performing. We bounced along to the rhythm of the Stereo MCs' song "Connected", trying to catch the camera whenever it cut to the audience.

"This is so fun!" shouted Saby.

As the song ended, we spotted another illuminated stage with a band waiting to start. We hurried over.

"Oh wow! It's Crowded House!" I shrieked.

"Get to the front, Lisa—see if the lead singer recognises you!" Lynn laughed.

Watching their flawless performance of "Only Natural", I reflected on the moment, seven months earlier, when the singer had spoken to me outside the Langham Hilton Hotel—and I had no clue who he was!

The rest of the evening was a mix of live studio performances, video clips, and satellite links. We dashed to the front of each stage whenever we could, hoping to appear on camera.

The thrill of the experience left us on a high for days, and when our episode aired, we had a great time trying to spot ourselves, though we only managed a couple of brief glimpses from a distance. When Michelle handed us tickets to more *Top of the Pops* recordings, we jumped at the chance to return.

After a couple more trips, word spread among our friends, and Michelle soon found herself supplying tickets to an ever-growing circle. Before long, we descended on the *Top of the Pops* studios like a small army, buzzing at the thought of seeing bands—and ourselves—on TV.

"Listen up, everyone," the floor manager called out. "We're trying something new tonight. Before the show begins, we'll play some music and film the crowd. Give us your best dance moves when the cameras come around."

We exchanged wide-eyed looks.

"Well," our friend Chris grinned, clapping his hands, "lucky I perfected my running man last night."

"Ha! Don't forget the lawn mower man too," I teased.

"I'll stick with big fish, little fish, cardboard box," Michelle laughed.

Ushered into the studio, we took our positions.

"Aaaand... action!" bellowed the director.

The music kicked in, and we went for it. Michelle and Lynn threw themselves into their big fish, little fish routine, while the rest of us—led by Chris—launched into a chaotic blend of lawn mower and running man. When the cameras swung our way, we cranked it up, limbs flying, giving it everything we had.

"And thank you, everybody! You can relax now," came the director's voice, followed by polite applause from the crew.

"I'm boiling now! That was so exhausting!" Saby panted.

"You're not wrong," I said, catching my breath. "Imagine how cool it'll look when this airs though!"

The lights shifted, the music dropped, and the show began. Once again, we dashed from stage to stage, catching Dina Carroll, Bryan Adams, Phil Collins, and more—fuelled by the thrill of it all.

The next evening, I sat with my family, excitement racing through the room as we watched the episode go to air. I couldn't wait to see our pre-show dance moves close up on camera.

"Oh... they didn't show us dancing," I muttered, as the presenter introduced the first act.

"Maybe they'll use the footage later," Dad suggested.

Fifteen minutes in, I suddenly spotted myself on screen and leapt to my feet.

"Look! I'm right there, at the edge of the stage—within touching distance of Bryan Adams!" I shrieked.

Just then, the phone rang. It was my friend Chris, who had been there too.

"Hey, you! You're famous!" he laughed.

"So are you!" I chuckled. "Though I'm not sure why they skipped our dancing."

"Maybe my running man and lawn mower moves were too much for the nation," Chris grinned.

"Or too good!" I shot back.

By age seventeen, being on TV had practically become a hobby for us. Michelle was our lifeline for tickets, but one day she broke the unfortunate news:

"Sorry," she sighed. "I haven't been able to get any more—I'll keep trying."

It was disappointing, though I knew demand was fierce. Free tickets to see big bands—with the chance of appearing on TV—were bound to be popular.

As the year turned, the thrill faded. We'd stopped asking Michelle. Some friends had already turned eighteen, eager to swap childhood for adulthood's privileges: driving, clubs, bars. It felt like a race, as if growing up were an exclusive club no one wanted to be left out of.

Then, in early February 1994, just when I thought our TV days were behind us, Michelle called.

"Lisa, I've got a load of tickets for *Top of the Pops* again!" she said breathlessly.

"I thought you couldn't get those anymore?" I replied.

"I couldn't get any for ages—Kylie and some other big acts caused a mad rush! But guess what? I've got some for next week. Are you coming?"

"Yes! Definitely! I'm not sure who else still wants to go, but I'm in!" I replied excitedly.

"Great! I'll ring around and let you know who's joining us," she promised.

To our delight, the old gang resurfaced at the first whiff of new tickets. Within a week, we were back together, laughing and chatting our way to London, the old excitement bubbling up as if no time had passed.

We saw some incredible acts that night—Cathy Dennis, The Cranberries, Shara Nelson, Suede. And as if that wasn't enough, I somehow ended up standing right next to presenter Simon Mayo during the outro. Surely this time I'd be on TV for at least a few precious seconds.

By the time we got back on the train, the adrenaline had burned off and hunger had set in.

"I'm starving," Michelle groaned. "Fancy a Burger King?"

"Definitely. All that dancing worked up an appetite," I laughed.

We charged through the restaurant doors and were delighted to find the place almost empty.

"Brilliant—no queues!" Saby grinned.

But as we reached the counter, the server glanced at us, froze, then spun on her heels and vanished out the back in a flash.

"What the...? Did she just see a ghost?" Lynn frowned.

Michelle and I locked eyes and immediately burst into laughter.

"Julie!" we squealed together.

Lynn looked baffled. "What's going on?"

"Oh, just a girl we went to school with," I explained. "She once told us we'd end up flipping burgers for a living."

"Looks like she took that career path herself," Michelle added with a smirk.

Thankfully, another staff member stepped in to serve us while Julie enjoyed an impromptu break from the counter.

The next evening, I waited anxiously for the final moments of *Top of the Pops*, eager to spot myself next to Simon Mayo, while my family crowded around the TV.

"Why aren't you looking at the camera?" my brother asked.

"Didn't feel right staring straight into the lens," I laughed. Maybe being on television wasn't as natural for me as I'd imagined.

That turned out to be my last trip to Top of the Pops. Not long after, the pull of adulthood—turning eighteen, college, first jobs—carried me away from those carefree rituals. Years passed, and the whirlwind of schooldays, gigs, and TV shows gradually gave way to the quieter rhythm of adult life—but those memories never lost their sparkle.

Years later, in the spring of 2003, I sat exhausted in my very first home, boxes stacked around me, Carl—my partner of eight years—slumped beside me on the sofa.

"I really needed this sit-down," he sighed.

"Same. I can't believe how much stuff we've got—it'll take forever to unpack," I said.

"Forget the boxes for now. How about a takeaway pizza?"

"Perfect," I smiled.

When it arrived, we settled back on the sofa, cardboard lids for plates, television flickering in the background.

Carl flicked through the channels and stopped at *Top of the Pops Two*—an episode from the 90s, a perfect slice of nostalgia. I froze in disbelief as the familiar studio came into view.

"Oh my God," I gasped, dropping my slice of pizza into the box on my lap.

"Everything alright?" Carl asked, slightly concerned.

"No—it's me! I'm on TV!" I squealed.

And there it was—the grainy footage of me beside Simon Mayo, frozen forever in 1994. I hadn't seen it in nearly a decade, yet suddenly it filled the room.

I had to explain the whole story to Carl, and before long I was reminiscing, laughing, and describing tales about the friendships, music, and mischief that had shaped my teenage years.

Becoming a homeowner felt like I'd reached a major milestone, but that night, seeing my teenage self beside Simon Mayo reminded me that the real milestones were the memories—the gigs, the friends, the laughter that never fades.

Time moves on, but those moments stay with you—a reminder that growing up doesn't mean losing your spark for adventure. And as I soaked in those memories, one final thought made me grin: Julie was wrong. I didn't end up flipping burgers… I ended up on *Top of the Pops*.

THE CROOKED PATH TO LOVE

CHAPTER ONE
YOUNG LOVE

It was a warm July evening in the summer of 1980, and Charlotte was in high spirits—her long-awaited date with Robbie had finally arrived.

He wore his favourite navy and red striped rugby shirt, which she particularly liked to see him in. She hoped that he, too, would approve of her outfit—her favourite pink and white floral dress.

Dining al fresco, Charlotte beamed as she tried to keep the conversation light and engaging, adding bits of humour and trying her best to hide her shyness. Robbie's charm and cheeky nature had her completely captivated. So captivated, in fact, that she didn't notice Robbie pause mid-sentence, eyebrows lifting as he glanced at his plate.

"Hey! That's my plate!" Robbie said suddenly, sounding a little annoyed.

"Oh... I'm sorry!" she replied, mortified.

Caught up in the moment, Charlotte hadn't realised she'd mistakenly taken food from Robbie's plate. She felt her cheeks flush, praying the mishap wouldn't spoil their evening.

Luckily, he laughed it off, and before there could be any more awkwardness, their time together was interrupted by a familiar voice.

"Charlotte, it's time for Robbie to go home," called her mum from the kitchen window.

The spell of their little tea party broke. Robbie set down his plastic cup, brushing crumbs from his shorts before hopping off the tiny garden chair.

"Can't he stay a bit longer?" Charlotte whispered, disheartened.

"I'm afraid not; his mum's here to pick him up. You'll see him tomorrow," her mum said with a smile.

At the tender age of four, Charlotte had her future sorted: grow up with Robbie, marry him, live happily ever after. Now she just had to break the news to Robbie!

The next day at nursery, Charlotte spotted Robbie in the cloakroom. He smiled and handed her an envelope. She beamed with excitement—was it something special?

"Hey, Charlotte! You got one too!" smiled her best friend Daisy, tucking an identical envelope into her bag.

"What do you mean?" Charlotte asked.

"It's Robbie's birthday invite," Daisy clarified.

Charlotte forced a smile. She was happy, but slightly disappointed that the envelope wasn't something special meant just for her.

Weeks later, at Robbie's party, Charlotte was awed by his huge house. His mum greeted her warmly and led her to the garden, where kids swarmed a playhouse and trampoline.

"Happy birthday, Robbie!" Charlotte said, handing him her gift.

"Thanks," he muttered, adding it to a pile of other gifts before dashing off. Charlotte's excitement dimmed—she had hoped for a moment with him.

Despite not managing to sit next to Robbie during the party games or at the table, Charlotte tried to appreciate simply being in his company that afternoon. Even so, she felt a small pang of envy when Daisy settled into the seat beside him at the birthday tea.

As the party ended, Robbie's mum gave her a party bag. "Thanks for coming. Stay in touch, won't you?"

"Yes, we will," Charlotte's mum replied.

But Charlotte was concerned they wouldn't. She and Robbie would be at different schools soon. She clung to the hope of another playdate—one that never came.

CHAPTER TWO
GROWING UP

Charlotte immersed herself in school and enjoyed making lots of new friends. She found herself occasionally missing Robbie, though. None of the boys at her school quite compared to him; they were all very boisterous and didn't seem to know how to communicate with girls.

One morning, a few years into her primary schooling, Charlotte noticed an unfamiliar face sitting alone at a table in her classroom.

"Right, now, can we have a bit of hush, please, everyone," requested Charlotte's teacher, Miss Jones. "We have a new member of the class joining us today. Please will you all welcome Billy."

Charlotte exchanged quick glances with her friends, whose eyes lit up. The girls all began whispering and had to be quietened by the teacher.

Billy looked quite different from the other boys, who were scruffy and not too bothered about their appearance. In contrast, Billy was well dressed and well groomed; his light blonde hair and bright blue eyes set him apart from the others.

As the weeks rolled past, the appreciation for the new classmate continued. All the girls in the class had become obsessed with him, writing "I love Billy Brookes" on the palms of their hands.

"Have you got that written on your hands too, Charlotte?" enquired classmate Anthony, during assembly one morning.

"What? No way!" she replied, showing her perfectly clean hands to him.

He seemed semi-satisfied that at least one girl in the class wasn't fazed by the arrival of the new boy.

Secretly, Charlotte was as curious about Billy as the other girls—not that she'd ever admit it.

As Christmas approached, spirits were high in school. This was the term when all the fun stuff happened—Christmas decoration making, carol singing, rehearsals for the school play, and so on.

One December morning, during break time, Charlotte noticed Billy approaching her on the playground.

"Happy Christmas, Charlotte," he smiled, handing her a Christmas card he'd written.

A warm smile spread across her face as she took the card, grateful and a little fluttery inside. She had never received a Christmas card from a boy before but knew there was something special about Billy. He wasn't like the other boys; he had a soft and sensitive disposition.

As she opened the envelope and pulled out the card, she smiled when she saw Care Bears all over the front in a snowy scene. When she opened it, her eyes fixated on the word "Love" and the endless kisses. Suddenly, Robbie was a distant memory.

A few days later, Charlotte's best friend, Daisy, came running over in the playground, her face glowing with excitement.

"Guess what?! Billy and I are going out!" Daisy announced, practically bouncing on her heels.

"What? You mean as in boyfriend and girlfriend?" Charlotte asked, puzzled.

"Yes! Boyfriend and girlfriend," Daisy clarified, her grin widening.

"Oh..." Charlotte's voice trailed off, the weight of disappointment sinking in.

She had secretly hoped Billy would notice her instead. Daisy always seemed to attract attention so effortlessly—her bright blonde hair catching the light, her easy confidence drawing people in. Charlotte, with her darker hair and quieter manner, often felt overlooked in comparison.

Forcing a smile, she tried to appear happy for her friend, but a faint sense of rejection tugged at her heart. As the days went by, she couldn't help but notice how Daisy now spent more time laughing with Billy and less with her, and each time she saw them together, the pang of jealousy deepened just a little more.

At this age, however, relationships were fleeting—most "going out" arrangements only lasted a few weeks, as if they came with an invisible expiration date. True to form, Daisy and Billy's "romance" ended just two weeks later.

When Daisy sought comfort after the breakup, Charlotte did her best to console her, pushing aside her own conflicting emotions. But she wasn't prepared for what came next.

"Hey, Charlotte," called Jon, one of Billy's closest friends, as he approached her in class one afternoon. "Billy wanted me to ask if you'd go out with him."

Charlotte froze. "Oh. Oh, right. Um..." she hesitated, her mind racing. Why would he want *her*—plain, brown-haired Charlotte—when he'd just been with Daisy, with her perfect blonde hair and easy confidence?

"I don't think I can—it wouldn't be fair to Daisy," she finally replied, her voice unsure.

"Okay, I'll let him know," Jon said with a shrug, satisfied to have delivered the message.

As Jon walked away, Charlotte felt a pang of regret. She liked Billy, but disbelief lingered beneath the flattery. And if it *was* genuine, would it have been wrong to say yes, even though he had just broken up with her best friend? Her gut told her she'd done the right thing, even if her heart wasn't so sure.

For the rest of school, there was no further dating, though Charlotte never entirely forgot Billy.

CHAPTER THREE
BROADENING HORIZONS

It was early September 1987, and Charlotte felt a mix of excitement and trepidation as she prepared to start secondary school. The prospect of exploring new subjects and making new friends was thrilling, but the sheer size and buzz of her new school left her feeling a little overwhelmed.

For now, boys were the furthest thing from Charlotte's mind. Her first few months at secondary school were spent laughing with her new friends, often huddled together during break times, flicking through the latest teen magazines. They giggled over horoscopes and celebrity gossip, forging bonds that made the daunting new environment feel a little smaller.

Yet it didn't escape Charlotte's notice that relationships seemed to bloom—and fizzle out—with alarming frequency around the school. The dramatic fallout of teenage breakups, accompanied by tearful outbursts in corridors, became a recurring backdrop to her days.

One morning during tutor period, Charlotte caught sight of Peter, a classmate notorious for his juvenile antics. He was chatting animatedly with his friends, but his frequent glances in her direction left her feeling uneasy.

"Psst, Daisy—can you hear what he's saying? He's definitely talking about me," Charlotte muttered to her friend, her tone tinged with irritation.

Daisy leaned in, smirking. "He's bragging about his paper

round. Apparently, he's going to start delivering on your street."

Charlotte frowned. She didn't dislike Peter exactly, but his attempts to solidify his reputation as the class clown often made him the butt of the jokes rather than the source. His antics veered toward the immature, and she had little patience for his behaviour.

It wasn't long before Peter's attention became more intrusive. One day, Charlotte overheard him loudly sharing her house number, street name, and even her parents' car registration with the entire class. She was furious. The breach of her privacy felt invasive, and she resented having personal details shared so casually.

"I think he likes you," Daisy teased one afternoon, her grin growing wider. "I bet he gives you a Valentine's card next week!"

Charlotte groaned. The idea made her stomach churn. She wanted nothing to do with Peter, and the thought of him singling her out on Valentine's Day filled her with dread. Determined to avoid him, she resolved to stay aloof and ignore his attention-seeking behaviour.

The dreaded day arrived. Charlotte was relieved to find no sign of a card in her letterbox after Peter's morning paper round. She allowed herself a fleeting moment of peace—until she walked into the tutor room for registration later that morning.

Peter beckoned Daisy over to his desk with a smug grin, handing her something that immediately set Charlotte's nerves on edge. Daisy returned, smirking, a large red envelope clutched in her hand.

Oh no. Charlotte's heart sank. This was it.

The class fell silent, except for a few stifled giggles.

"I'm not taking that," Charlotte said firmly, her voice louder than intended.

"Yes, you are," Daisy shot back with a mischievous glint in her eye. She grabbed Charlotte's school bag and tried to stuff the envelope inside.

"Stop it!" Charlotte snapped, wrestling her bag away from Daisy. The two girls scuffled briefly, the class erupting in laughter as Charlotte's frustration grew. Even Peter joined in, his laughter cutting through the noise and making her cheeks burn with humiliation.

In one swift motion, Charlotte snatched the card from Daisy and tore it apart, her hands shaking with anger. Bits of the red envelope and its contents fluttered to the floor as the room fell silent. Gasps rippled through the class, followed by stunned whispers. No one had expected that.

Even Charlotte was taken aback by her own reaction. She hadn't planned to rip up the card, but the overwhelming anxiety of the situation had driven her to act impulsively.

Fortunately, the arrival of the teacher broke the tension,

redirecting everyone's attention. Charlotte quickly slid into her seat, her face flushed and her chest tight with embarrassment. The pieces of the card lay scattered around her, a vivid reminder of the morning's chaos.

For the rest of the day, Charlotte kept her head down, avoiding Peter's gaze. She knew she had to put the incident behind her, but deep down, the lingering embarrassment made it hard to forget.

In the weeks that followed, Charlotte stuck to ignoring Peter and, to her relief, he eventually got the message.

Some months later, Charlotte was sat around the dinner table with her family one evening, when her mum sparked an intriguing conversation.

"Oh, did you see in the local paper that Robbie's family are looking for volunteers for their charity?" her mum remarked casually.

"Robbie? As in Robbie-from-nursery Robbie?" Charlotte asked, her interest instantly piqued.

"Yes, that Robbie. His family are asking for help from the public. They even put their phone number in the paper so people can contact them directly," her mum replied.

Charlotte's curiosity was immediately stirred. After dinner, she grabbed the newspaper and flipped through the pages until she found the notice. Sure enough, there it was— Robbie's home phone number staring back at her. She stared at it, her mind racing. Should she call? Would he even remember her? And if he did, would he be happy to hear from her?

Unable to stop thinking about it, Charlotte took the newspaper to school the next day and shared the story with her friends during their break.

"I know Robbie! He went to my primary school," her classmate Meghan chimed in after overhearing the conversation.

Charlotte's excitement grew. She eagerly shared how she had known him as a young child and bombarded Meghan with questions about what Robbie was up to now.

By the end of the school day, Charlotte, Daisy and Meghan found themselves huddled together in a cramped phone booth. With a mix of nerves and anticipation, Charlotte dialled Robbie's number.

"Hi, can I speak to Robbie, please?" she asked, her voice trembling slightly as an older male answered the call.

Moments later, Robbie came to the phone.

"Hi Robbie, it's Charlotte. Not sure if you remember me, but we went to nursery together," she said, her voice bright with hope.

"Oh, hi. Yes, I remember you," Robbie replied, sounding slightly reserved but polite.

They chatted briefly, exchanging small talk before

Charlotte worked up the courage to give him her home phone number. To her delight, Robbie promised to call her over the weekend. She hung up the phone buzzing with excitement.

The weekend came and went with no call, sadly, turning her enthusiasm into disappointment. *Maybe he didn't really want to see me,* she thought. *Maybe he was just being polite.*

Then, a couple of weeks later, the phone rang unexpectedly.

"Charlotte! Phone for you—it's Robbie!" her mum called out.

Robbie? Charlotte thought, her heart skipping a beat as she dashed down the stairs and grabbed the receiver.

"Hi, Charlotte, it's Robbie," he said. "I was wondering if you'd like to meet up in town this Saturday. We could grab something to eat?"

Charlotte's heart raced with excitement. "Yes, that sounds great!" she agreed, arranging to meet him outside a fast-food restaurant in the town centre at noon.

"Oh, how sweet that you two are meeting up—and that he's taking you out for lunch!" her mum said, grinning with delight when Charlotte told her.

"Yes, I guess so," Charlotte replied, but her tone lacked enthusiasm.

"What's wrong? Don't you want to see him?" her mum asked, sensing her hesitation.

"It's just... his voice sounded so different from when I first spoke to him. Almost like it was a completely different person," Charlotte admitted, her brow furrowed with doubt.

Despite her misgivings, Charlotte couldn't resist the chance to reconnect with Robbie. She decided to go and meet him anyway.

That Saturday, Charlotte stood outside the restaurant, scanning the crowd. Minutes turned into half an hour, then forty minutes. Robbie never showed.

Heart sinking, Charlotte finally gave up and left. As she walked home, a knot of disappointment tightened in her chest. Had he changed his mind? Or were her suspicions correct—that the second call had been from someone else entirely, pretending to be Robbie for a laugh?

Whatever the truth, Charlotte never had any further contact with Robbie and accepted she would never see him again.

She resolved to put the whole experience behind her. Robbie was a part of her past, and she wouldn't let the disappointment overshadow her present.

Some months later, as she walked out of school one afternoon, Charlotte reached into her pocket and discovered a folded note, written on a torn page from a maths book. Opening it, she realised it was from a boy in her maths class.

The note was filled with compliments about her appearance and expressions of admiration.

Charlotte was completely taken aback. This boy had never spoken to her, never even glanced her way during lessons. Part of her was flattered, but another part was deeply suspicious—particularly after the Robbie incident.

In the end, she convinced herself it had to be a prank—someone impersonating him as part of a cruel joke. If that was the case, it was frustrating, but since she wasn't remotely attracted to him anyway, she tried to put it out of her mind.

With no follow-up from the maths love note, Charlotte breathed a quiet sigh of relief. The months that followed passed uneventfully; she kept her head down, content to stay out of the spotlight and let the whole thing fade into memory. From time to time, she caught the occasional glance from one of the quieter boys in her class, but she thought little of it.

Then came the next Valentine's Day. That same boy—Sehail—left a card on her desk, a simple note with a small, neatly written poem. For a moment, Charlotte blinked at the handwriting, a flicker of memory surfacing: an evening months earlier at his house, when Meghan's friend—Sehail's sister—had invited them over to play. She remembered the soft rustle of a tablecloth brushing her shoulder, the muffled giggles of hide-and-seek, and Sehail grinning at her in the dim space beneath the table as if perfectly content to be there with her.

Oh no, she realised, *he must have developed feelings for me from that moment.* The card and poem were sweet enough, but she didn't feel the same way, and the attention left her awkward and uncertain. Still, compared to the chaos of the last Valentine's incident, she managed it gracefully— quietly, maturely, and without a scene. Rather than respond, she simply tucked the card away, letting it fade quietly.

By the time she reached her final year at school, Charlotte had mastered the art of keeping a low profile. She focused on friends, schoolwork, and the usual small dramas— completely unaware that the year ahead might shake up her quiet little world in the most unexpected ways.

CHAPTER FOUR
ROAD TO HEARTBREAK

In her final year of school, Charlotte grew close to a new friend she'd met in English lessons—a fun-loving girl named Sally, who'd been seated next to her. One morning as she queued outside her English classroom, Sally approached her, brimming with excitement.

"Hey Charl, can you help me with my project, please?" Sally asked, clasping her hands together.

"What's it about?" Charlotte asked, raising an eyebrow.

"It's a school dating service! I've set up a computer algorithm to match people based on their interests and personalities. Please say yes—you'd really be helping me out." Sally explained eagerly.

Charlotte blinked in disbelief. "A dating service? How's that even a project? Sorry, Sally—there aren't any boys in this school I like, so it'd be pointless," she insisted, shaking her head.

But Sally was relentless. After five minutes of pleading, she convinced Charlotte to participate, framing it as a massive favour. Though reluctantly agreeing, Charlotte regretted it almost immediately.

A week later, Sally bounded up to her at lunchtime, grinning triumphantly.

"I've got your results!" she announced. "You've been matched! Well, twice, actually."

Charlotte groaned. "Oh, no. Do I even want to know?"

"The first one is Jamie," Sally said, practically bouncing with excitement.

"Jamie?" Charlotte's stomach sank. "You've got to be joking. He hates me—and I hate him, for that matter! How did your algorithm mess that up? Please don't tell him he's been matched with me."

"I'm sorry, but I have to deliver the results fairly," replied Sally.

Charlotte felt a wave of discomfort wash over her. The last thing she wanted was for Jamie to know they'd been matched.

"Do you want to hear the second one?" Sally asked, her grin widening.

"Not really," Charlotte muttered, already dreading the answer.

"It's David!" Sally blurted, unable to contain her excitement.

Charlotte blinked in confusion. "David who? There's more than one in our year."

"David McKenzie," Sally clarified. "You know—the one in our English class?"

Charlotte paused, letting the name settle in her mind. She hadn't given much thought to David before, but now found herself intrigued. He was attractive, seemed mature, and, from what little she knew of him, came across as a genuinely nice guy.

"He's asked for your home phone number. Is that okay?" Sally asked.

Charlotte's heart skipped. "Wait—you told him about the match before speaking to me?"

Sally winced. "Sorry—I ran into him this morning. But hey, the good news is he said he's interested."

"He did?" Charlotte felt her cheeks flush. "Oh, wow. Um, okay. Sure, you can give him my number."

As Sally walked away, Charlotte stood rooted to the spot, her mind racing. She hadn't expected this turn of events, and the thought of David being interested in her left her slightly dazed—but undeniably curious.

Days passed with no word from David, and Charlotte started to wonder if he'd lost interest. Then, one evening, her mum called upstairs.

"Charlotte, there's someone on the phone for you. It's David."

Charlotte's heart raced. So, he did want to talk to her. Taking a few deep breaths to steady herself, she picked up the receiver.

What followed was an hour and a half of easy, enjoyable conversation. David was charming, funny, and surprisingly easy to talk to; it was as if she'd known him for years. By the end of the call, they'd made plans to go to the cinema the following week.

The weeks that followed were blissful—after their cinema trip, there were bike rides, study sessions, and lazy afternoons hanging out. Charlotte felt completely at ease in his company. She genuinely enjoyed being around him.

"So?" Sally asked one day, her face lighting up with excitement. "What's the deal? Are you two, like, officially a couple now?"

"Well... not exactly," Charlotte replied with a small smile. "But we do like each other."

Word of their connection spread quickly through school, and soon, friends from both sides were brimming with questions, eager for confirmation that they were officially boyfriend and girlfriend. The pressure was intense, and Charlotte found herself hesitating.

Despite their strong connection, Charlotte avoided labelling their relationship. Over the next few months, they grew close and continued to spend time together, but it stayed undefined.

Then came the news that David wouldn't be staying on at the school for sixth form. He had decided to enrol at a local college instead. Charlotte's stomach dropped. Fear gripped her—he's going to meet someone else.

And, of course, that's exactly what happened that autumn...

"Hey, Charlotte!" Sally called out across the sixth-form common room one morning. Her voice carried a note of hesitation. "I need to tell you something... I'm really sorry, but I just heard that David is seeing someone."

Charlotte froze. "What? Are you sure?" she asked, feeling a lump form in her throat.

"Yes," Sally said sympathetically. "He's dating a girl from college; apparently, he's been seeing her for the last two weeks."

Charlotte forced a tight smile. "It's okay. We were never really together, so I guess it was inevitable."

But as the day went on, the news felt harder and harder to bear. Other people, assuming she didn't already know, kept approaching her to share the same information. By the time the day was over, she was exhausted from hearing it. Her chest felt tight, as though there was a physical ache where her heart should be.

So, I guess this is what heartache feels like, she thought. *Why didn't I tell him how I felt?*

For a while, she held on to the selfish hope that David's new relationship would fizzle out. Maybe, if it ended, she could finally muster the courage to share her feelings with him.

The following weeks were rough, but slowly, Charlotte began to focus on her studies again. She spent more time with her friends, and though the pain lingered, it eventually softened.

Months later, she heard that David was single again. The news ignited a flicker of hope. She decided to invite him over and finally tell him how she felt.

When David arrived at her door, she tried to steady her nerves. "Thanks for coming over," she said. "Come in—sit down. I need to ask you something."

"Sure, what's up?" he replied, sitting on the sofa.

"How do you feel about me?" Charlotte asked, trying to sound casual.

David leaned back slightly, his expression unreadable. "Well, you're a good friend," he said with a smile.

Her heart sank. "And that's it?" she pressed, trying to hide the panic rising within her.

"Yeah, I'm sorry," he said, looking awkward.

There was a long pause. Charlotte was quite taken aback by the response.

"Sorry, Charlotte, but I'm going to need to go—I've got to be at work in half an hour. Maybe we can talk again later this week?" he suggested, standing up and looking eager to leave.

She nodded, forcing a smile. "Okay. Thanks for coming by."

As David walked away, Charlotte closed the door behind him and leaned against it, her heart shattering.

She felt a rush of shock, humiliation, and quiet heartache. For days, she felt hollow and unsure what to do next. This wasn't like the pain of seeing him with someone else; it was rejection—plain and undeniable—something she needed time to accept.

The days after David's rejection passed in a haze. Charlotte went through the motions—lessons, coursework, sleep—but everything felt flat. She kept replaying their conversation, wondering if she'd imagined things. The Valentine's card he'd given her, the dance at the school disco—had she just read too much into it all?

I just need to forget about him, she thought one evening, staring at her untouched dinner.

Sally must have sensed it too. A few days later, she called with a plan.

"Come out with us this weekend," she urged. "We'll go to town, have some fun. No more moping."

Charlotte hesitated. The last thing she felt like doing was socialising, but maybe Sally was right. Maybe she needed a night out.

And so, that Saturday evening, she found herself in a quiet pub with Sally and Meghan, trying to shake off the lingering gloom that had settled over her.

"Do you think we should have picked somewhere else? It's pretty dead in here," Meghan remarked, glancing around the quiet pub.

"I think you're forgetting—we're only seventeen!" Sally reminded her with a grin. "This is one of the few places that doesn't check ID."

Before Meghan could respond, the door burst open, and a group of seven or eight young men strolled in, their laughter and energy instantly lifting the mood of the room.

"I think your luck might be about to change, Charlotte," Meghan teased, nudging her friend as her eyes followed the newcomers.

The young men ordered drinks at the bar, their smiles and animated conversation filling the space. It wasn't long before they noticed Charlotte and her friends and made their way over, asking if they could join them.

After an exchange of introductions, the group proudly revealed that they were Army cadets. Sally's eyes sparkled with interest at the announcement. One cadet in particular, Danny, seemed drawn to Charlotte. His easy charm, sharp wit, and friendly northern accent captivated her, and she found herself laughing along with his jokes and stories. By the end of the evening, the two had exchanged phone numbers.

Charlotte left the pub with her head spinning. She wasn't entirely sure if she was attracted to Danny, but the attention he gave her was flattering and gave her a much-needed confidence boost.

Danny called her the very next day, and the following weekend, they met up at a party one of her friends was hosting. They spent the evening chatting and laughing, and within days, he was visiting her at her home.

Though Charlotte enjoyed his company, she began to feel uneasy about how keen he seemed. She wasn't sure if her feelings for him matched his enthusiasm. Not wanting to lead him on, she debated whether to gently set boundaries or wait and see how things progressed.

A few weeks later, however, Danny shared some news that changed everything. "I'm being deployed to Iraq," he told her.

Charlotte hadn't expected this. Suddenly, the thought of him leaving left her feeling a little deflated.

"I'll write to you," Danny promised. "Once I have my address, I'll send it to you. You can get free "blueys" from the post office to write back to me."

"Blueys?" Charlotte asked, confused.

"They're blue airmail letter forms," Danny explained with a smile. "You can pick them up for free, and postage is already paid."

In the months that followed, Charlotte and Danny exchanged numerous blueys. His letters were filled with humour and charm, and they never failed to bring a smile to her face. However, as time passed, the letters became less frequent. Eventually, they stopped altogether, and the two quietly drifted apart.

Charlotte felt a twinge of sadness at losing contact but acknowledged that her feelings for Danny had never run deep enough to pursue something more serious. Despite that, his brief presence in her life had given her a renewed sense of confidence and a reminder of her own worth.

With this newfound self-assurance, Charlotte refocused on spending time with friends, enjoying her freedom, and living in the moment. She was certain that when the time was right, the right person would come along.

CHAPTER FIVE
IRRESISTIBLE

As Charlotte approached the end of her teenage years, her newfound confidence—combined with a new wardrobe and a makeover from Sally—seemed to launch her into an entirely new light. Suddenly, she was attracting attention wherever she went: college, work, nights out, or even casual strolls through the shops on her lunch break. It was as if a superpower had been thrust upon her—she had become irresistible.

Charlotte's friendly nature also drew people to her, but her naivety sometimes led her into unexpected situations, as she discovered shortly into her working life. After leaving sixth form, she had landed an admin job at the local university, where she often interacted with students, postgraduates, and lecturers.

One afternoon, Graham, a friendly postgrad, asked, "Do you play guitar?"

Charlotte's interest piqued immediately. "Kind of," she replied, smiling.

"I've just bought a new twelve-string—it's in my office. Fancy stopping by at lunch to give it a go?" he suggested.

"Yes, that would be amazing! I'll see you later," Charlotte replied, genuinely excited.

When lunchtime came, Charlotte made her way to

Graham's office, where he eagerly presented her with the guitar. It was sleek, shiny, and had a beautifully rich sound. She happily strummed a few chords, enjoying the moment and a discussion about favourite bands and songs, until Graham hesitated and asked, "Would you like to go out sometime?"

Charlotte's stomach sank. "Oh... I'm not looking to date anyone right now," she said, wincing at the awkwardness. He looked deflated, so she suggested grabbing a drink as friends to ease the tension.

Before long, another male postgrad began leaving expensive gifts on her desk—silk scarves among them. At first, she assumed they were harmless souvenirs from his overseas trips, but unease crept in when she found a handwritten note asking to meet in his office. When she didn't show, he came looking for her, visibly disappointed. She made a quick excuse, but from then on, she kept her distance.

Eighteen months later, Charlotte felt she had outgrown her first job and decided to move to a new role at a different company. Her new boss seemed impressed with her, even offering her any hourly rate she wanted, which made her feel immediately valued. But as the months passed, his behaviour began to shift—lunch invitations, offers of lifts home, and obvious disappointment whenever she declined.

At the office Christmas party, he made a beeline for her and asked for a dance. Uncomfortable but reluctant to cause a scene, she agreed. When she returned to her seat, her colleague Jackie nearly choked on her drink. "Wow... I think the boss has taken a real shine to you," she said, raising her eyebrows.

Charlotte flushed as others laughed and agreed—she hadn't realised her brief dance could spark so much speculation.

Back in the office, she kept things professional, but the lunch invites from her boss persisted. When she consistently declined, he began nitpicking her work. The atmosphere turned tense and unpleasant. Feeling unfairly treated and deeply uncomfortable, Charlotte handed in her notice. She was sad to leave behind a job and colleagues she was fond of, but welcomed a fresh start at her new workplace across town, where she would be working alongside her friend Meghan.

Although Charlotte's warm and friendly demeanour was simply who she was, she consciously began treading more carefully around male colleagues to avoid any unwelcome attention. At least in her personal life, she could relax and truly be herself. Weekends became her sanctuary, filled with laughter and a vibrant social life.

"Mum, just so you know, Chris is coming over later—we're going to watch a movie. Oh, and I'm expecting a call from Ryan. I need to arrange to give him his guitar back," she said one evening, smiling.

"Oh, okay," her mum replied. "By the way, did you see the message on the board? Nick called earlier while you were out.

He said he'd call again later."

Charlotte frowned slightly. "Hmm, okay. I expect he's ringing to chase up whether I'm joining him and his parents for dinner tomorrow night. I haven't given him an answer yet."

"Why would you be having dinner with him and his parents? You're not his girlfriend," her mum remarked, puzzled.

"I know. Sally introduced me to him because we both play guitar. We've met a couple of times as friends, but he keeps inviting me to things—like the cinema or dinner in London with his parents. I'm not sure why," Charlotte said thoughtfully.

"Well, you do tend to dress up when you go to see him. No wonder he's getting the wrong idea," her mum pointed out.

"I literally wear a polo-neck jumper and jeans! His house is always freezing—I'm not exactly dressing to impress," she protested.

"You're so stupid!" shouted her brother, who had been listening from the next room.

"What? What do you mean?" Charlotte demanded, confused.

"You!" he snapped. "You've got all these male friends, and you're pretending you don't realise they all want to date you!"

Charlotte froze, her brother's words stopping her in her tracks. Was he right? Had she been blind to the intentions of her male friends? She hadn't meant to mislead anyone—she was just enjoying the company of both male and female friends alike.

His comment stung, but it made her pause for reflection. She didn't want to hurt anyone's feelings, so she resolved to make her intentions clearer whenever she had the chance. It wasn't about changing who she was—it was about being considerate and ensuring her friends understood the boundaries.

A couple of months later, Charlotte and her friend, Daisy decided it was time to let off a bit of steam. The pair boarded a plane to Ibiza for a much-needed girls' getaway.

Ibiza was teeming with young Brits, ready to let loose and party around the clock. Charlotte wasn't looking for a wild holiday necessarily, but she was up for some fun—drinking, dancing, and maybe even a foam party or two.

Daisy was more on the wilder side. A couple of times, Charlotte awoke to notes from her saying she'd gone out to an all-night party. When Daisy rolled back into the apartment at 10 a.m., she wasn't exactly thrilled with Charlotte's suggestion of heading straight to the beach.

It was Charlotte and Daisy's first holiday abroad without parents, and they relished the freedom. Days were spent relaxing on the beach, while nights were a blur of music, laughter, and neon-lit clubs.

One night at a club, Charlotte noticed a boy who looked strikingly like David McKenzie—the boy she was fond of at school. As he danced toward her with a smile, a fleeting thought of the boy she once believed was "the one" crossed her mind.

"What's wrong? Don't you like my moves?" the boy teased, grinning as he tried to impress her.

Charlotte offered him a polite smile but kept scanning the room for Daisy, who had popped to the toilet ten minutes earlier. She suddenly spotted her chatting with two boys across the dance floor, so headed over to them.

"Hey, Charlotte! We've been invited back to Darren's apartment for drinks," Daisy said, beckoning Charlotte closer.

Charlotte hesitated. She felt uneasy about the invitation but didn't want to separate from Daisy—bold, self-assured, and always in control. Sticking with her felt safe.

At Darren's apartment, they drank and chatted casually until Darren's friend announced he was heading to bed. Suddenly, Charlotte felt like a third wheel.

"I'm feeling pretty tired too—I think I'll leave you two to it," Charlotte said to Daisy, standing to go.

Before Daisy could respond, Darren blocked Charlotte's path.

"No, don't leave," he insisted, his tone shifting from friendly to forceful as he grabbed Charlotte's arm. "Well, I'm not letting you leave unless you kiss me first."

Charlotte's stomach dropped as panic set in. She glanced at Daisy, hoping for support, but Daisy froze, staring back blankly.

"Daisy?!" Charlotte pleaded, desperate for help.

Daisy said nothing. A flicker of something—hurt, maybe even jealousy—crossed her face. She wasn't used to being the one overlooked, especially not for Charlotte. Charlotte was shocked her friend wasn't stepping in.

"Just one kiss, and I'll let you go," Darren pressed, his grip tightening.

Charlotte felt powerless. Trembling, she leaned forward and let him kiss her. True to his word, he released her. Without hesitation, Charlotte and Daisy bolted from the apartment, hailing a taxi back to their side of town.

Though they arrived back safely, the experience left Charlotte shaken. Suddenly, unwanted attention had shifted from bothersome to frightening.

Charlotte didn't go out much on her return home—staying in felt safer. But when her friend, Sally's birthday approached, she knew she'd have to resume her social life.

On the evening of the celebration, Charlotte, Daisy and Meghan took a taxi to Sally's chosen pub. As they walked in, they were greeted by Sally, her boyfriend Mike, and a long table of mutual friends.

Charlotte found herself enjoying the evening—chatting, drinking, and catching up with everyone. The atmosphere was lively and relaxed.

Partway through the night, Mike's phone rang, and he stepped aside to take the call, which seemed to drag on forever.

"Oh, it's Mike's brother, Matthew," Sally explained with a smile. "They've reconnected recently. Matthew was living in the States for years, but now he's back in the UK, and they've been catching up loads. It's lovely."

Eventually, Mike handed the phone to Sally, who chatted warmly for a few moments before unexpectedly turning to Charlotte.

"Here, Charlotte, talk to Matthew—he's really nice," she insisted, passing the phone over.

Caught off guard, Charlotte hesitated but took the phone. "Hi, I'm Charlotte, Sally's friend. We're just out celebrating her birthday," she said, trying to sound natural.

To her surprise, Charlotte found herself enjoying the conversation. Matthew, though a stranger, had a friendly demeanour and a charming American accent. After some polite small talk, she handed the phone back to Sally, feeling a little amused by the unusual interaction.

The following week, while out with Sally and friends again, a similar situation unfolded. Mike took a call from Matthew, and after some chatting, it was passed to Charlotte once more. This time, feeling a bit more relaxed and merry, she chatted with Matthew longer.

When she hung up, Sally leaned in eagerly. "What did he say, Charlotte?"

"He said he's staying with his parents next weekend and asked if I'd like to meet him at their local pub next Saturday evening," Charlotte replied, her voice tinged with uncertainty.

"Aww, that's amazing! He's so lovely—and come on, he's Mike's brother, so you know he's bound to be gorgeous!" Sally teased, throwing her arms around Mike.

Charlotte felt a mix of excitement and nerves. Matthew's voice had been so appealing on the phone—surely he would be as appealing in person.

When the following Saturday arrived, Charlotte got dressed up, caught a ride into town, and boarded a train to the next town. As she sat on the train, nerves crept in. *What am I doing? I'm catching a train to meet a stranger. This is basically a blind date. What if I don't like him? What if he doesn't like me?*

The pub was only a short walk from the station, but as she stood outside, doubt settled in. *What if I'm stood up?* she wondered, remembering the Robbie incident years earlier.

She watched people pass by—some entering the pub, others continuing on their way. Her nerves began to spiral. Suddenly, a man approached, looking a bit lost.

He caught her eye and smiled briefly before speaking. "Charlotte?"

Her heart sank. He knew her name. This had to be Matthew.

"Oh, hi—nice to finally meet you," she replied, forcing a smile while inwardly suppressing her disappointment.

Matthew was nothing like she'd imagined. He bore no resemblance to Mike, and Charlotte knew immediately she wasn't attracted to him. Still, she resolved to go through with the evening.

To her surprise, she really enjoyed his company. Matthew was charming, funny, and easy to talk to, and she did have a pleasant time, but as her last train home approached, she used it as a reason to leave.

Matthew walked her to the train platform, where she quickly boarded, giving him only a polite smile and wave through the glass as the train doors closed. Relieved, she sank into a seat and exhaled deeply.

The next day, Matthew called, inviting her to meet him in London over the Bank Holiday. She hesitated, unsure of her feelings, but eventually decided to go ahead.

When she stepped off the train at Paddington Station the following Monday morning, he greeted her warmly. "Hey, Charlotte! Great to see you!"

"Good to see you too! What did you have in mind for

today?" she asked.

"Well, I thought we could wander through Covent Garden, maybe grab a bite to eat," he began, then suddenly stopped, a worried look crossing his face.

"Oh... I just remembered—I left a heater on in my flat. I need to pop back and turn it off. Are you okay if we do that first?"

Charlotte froze, caught off guard. The request made her uneasy. She didn't know him that well, and the idea of going to his flat felt wrong. Flashbacks of her Ibiza experience rushed back, filling her with dread.

"I'm really sorry, Matthew—I don't think I can come with you," she said finally, her voice apologetic but firm. She explained she didn't have much time before needing to head home and suggested they reschedule.

The following evening, Matthew left her a voicemail, and although she felt guilty doing so, she didn't call back. He made no further attempts to contact her, much to her relief.

CHAPTER SIX
"THE ONE"

Charlotte considered herself lucky—she never felt the desperate need to be in a relationship. She had spent time in the past worrying about the wrong people liking her and the right people ignoring her, but those days felt behind her. Now, she was content on her own. While some of her friends seemed to jump from one partner to the next, as though they couldn't bear to be alone, Charlotte appreciated the freedom of being single. It also made it easier to maintain her close friendships with both men and women, all of whom she deeply valued.

Over time, Charlotte's circle of friends naturally expanded. Friends often introduced new people into her social group, and somehow, everyone always seemed to hit it off effortlessly. One evening at their local pub, Meghan had invited one of the new office interns—Shaun. He was a little younger than everyone else in the group, but his warm personality and razor-sharp sense of humour instantly won everyone over.

Charlotte had only met Shaun briefly in the office, but as she got to know him better, she realised how much they clicked. They shared the same sense of humour and began pranking each other at work with fake calls, which sometimes got out of hand, but they could also talk for hours about music, travel, and the paranormal. She found his company easy and comforting—he was the kind of person who really listened.

As months passed, Charlotte and Shaun grew close. They met for lunch at work often, sharing little details about their days, and confiding in each other about things they didn't always tell others. Charlotte valued the friendship deeply, while Shaun viewed the lengthy chats, inside jokes, and small gestures as something more meaningful—perhaps the start of something deeper.

One evening at their favourite nightclub, Charlotte shared a few drinks with her usual friend group, including Shaun, who patiently talked her through a tricky work problem. She smiled, leaning closer and looping an arm around his shoulders.

"You always know how to make me feel better, Shaun—I really do love you for that," she said warmly.

He froze for a moment, studying her expression, then leaned in closer and kissed her on the lips.

Charlotte was taken aback. She hadn't expected that to happen, but with everyone in high spirits, a little tipsy, and enjoying the night, she decided not to dwell on it.

The next morning, Charlotte woke to the faint hum of cars in the distance, her head pounding slightly from the night before. As she blinked against the daylight streaming through the curtains, flashes of the evening replayed in her mind—the laughter, the music, Shaun's easy company, and then... the kiss. A sinking feeling settled in her stomach. Had she somehow led Shaun to believe there was something more between them?

Charlotte spent the rest of the morning wrestling with her thoughts, replaying the moment over and over. Maybe she was overthinking it. Maybe Shaun saw it as nothing more than a drunken slip-up, just like *she* had. But a nagging doubt lingered What if he didn't? She considered calling him, clearing the air before things got awkward—but before she could make a decision, a knock at the door made her jump. When she opened it, she found Shaun standing there, smiling.

"Hi, Charlotte—I hope you don't mind me dropping by," he began, smiling shyly. "I just wanted to talk about last night."

His words—and the look in his eyes—hit her like a freight train. Charlotte smiled and nodded, but inside, panic flared; she had no idea how to respond.

Somehow, she managed to brush over it, steering the conversation toward Meghan's upcoming birthday party, all the while praying he wouldn't bring it back to the night before.

Her brother's teasing words about her being oblivious to male attention echoed in her mind. *I really am clueless sometimes,* she thought regretfully.

Over the next couple of weeks, Charlotte continued to avoid any discussions about pursuing anything serious with Shaun, instead focusing just on enjoying time with him and the rest of their friend group all together. She valued their dynamic and didn't want to disrupt it.

Soon after, it was time for Meghan's twenty-first birthday party. Charlotte loved a good celebration and was excited to join in the fun at Meghan's house alongside their mutual friends.

"Happy birthday, Meg!" Charlotte and the others cheered as she opened the door.

"Hi everyone! Thanks! Come on in!" Meghan replied, grinning with a drink already in hand.

As they filed inside, setting their gifts and cards on the dining table, Charlotte greeted Shaun—then noticed an unfamiliar but cheerful-looking face standing beside him.

"Oh—everyone, this is Alex, by the way," Meghan announced, gesturing toward him. "He's one of Shaun's housemates."

"Nice to meet you, Alex," Charlotte said with a smile, before adding with a playful laugh, "Right! Now, where's the wine?"

The party turned out to be a roaring success. The house was alive with music, dancing, singing, and plenty of laughter. By 4:30 a.m., the festivities finally wound down, and Charlotte and a handful of others ended up crashing in the dining room.

Running on just a couple of hours' sleep, Charlotte and her friends groggily left at 6:30 a.m., catching the first bus home. Somewhere along the route, hunger won out, and they hopped off at a nearby fast-food place for a much-needed breakfast. It was there that Daisy made an unexpected admission.

"Hey Charlotte, I'm thinking of asking Alex out," she confided.

Charlotte paused for a moment, placing the name in her mind.

"Oh, Shaun's housemate, you mean?" she asked. Daisy nodded.

"Yeah, why not? I didn't speak to him much, but he seems nice," Charlotte said with a smile.

In the weeks that followed, Charlotte noticed Alex tagging along on their regular nights out. Though nothing seemed to develop between him and Daisy at first, he quickly became a fully integrated member of the group, his cheeky sense of humour and natural ability to entertain making him easy to welcome.

At first, Charlotte hadn't thought much of Alex beyond being one of Shaun's friendly housemates. But over time, she began to notice a change: she looked forward to seeing him, replayed their conversations in her head, and laughed at things he'd said long after he'd left. It wasn't just his happy-go-lucky personality or boyish charm that drew her in—it was the effortless ease between them, as if they'd known each other for years. Yet she couldn't tell if he felt the same way, and of course, she didn't want to tread on Daisy's toes.

One evening, beneath the glow of the nightclub lights, Charlotte and Alex found themselves alone at the bar. She'd been feeling low lately, a cloud she couldn't shake, unsure how to lift herself out of it.

"I know we haven't known each other long, Charlotte," Alex said, his voice quiet but steady, "but if anything ever happened to you... I'd be really upset. I mean it."

Charlotte froze, the words hitting her harder than she expected. Was he trying to comfort her—or make her heart skip a beat?

"Thank you," she murmured, surprised by how much his words affected her. She then found herself admitting something that had been on her mind. "You know, I'm actually a big fan of yours, but I feel bad telling you this—I know Daisy likes you."

Alex looked surprised, but a pleased smile spread across his face. "Daisy's a nice girl, but not my type—it's you I'm drawn to."

Charlotte blushed, glancing briefly at the floor. Wanting to escape the noise and continue talking, they decided to leave the club for a late-night stroll.

After a long evening of walking and talking, Alex accompanied Charlotte all the way home. As she hugged him goodbye, she lingered—holding onto him just a little longer than usual. In that moment, everything felt right, as if it had been meant to be. It felt as if the stars had aligned, and everything was falling perfectly into place.

The next day, he called, eager but cautious. "Hey, Charlotte—how are you? How do you feel about last night?" Alex asked, his voice carrying a hint of uncertainty.

"I'm good, thanks. I had a great time last night. I had no idea you liked me, but I'm really glad," Charlotte replied.

Alex let out a relieved laugh. "I'm so happy to hear that. When can I see you again?"

Her stomach tightened. He wanted to see her as soon as possible, which was sweet—but was this moving too fast?

"Well, I'll be out again next Saturday. I'll see you at the club?" she offered, needing time to process her feelings.

She was torn. She really liked Alex, but she didn't want to rush things and risk it falling apart. And then there was Shaun—Alex's housemate and her friend—whose friendship she valued greatly. On top of that, Daisy also liked Alex, and the thought of hurting her made Charlotte hesitate even more. She couldn't help but wonder how a relationship with Alex might affect both her bond with Shaun and her friendship with Daisy.

She had a lot to think about, including the lingering regret of how she had hesitated with David—long enough for him to find someone else then change his mind about her altogether. She didn't want to make the same mistake again. Maybe it was time to silence her doubts and trust her instincts.

In no time, Charlotte's bond with Alex grew too strong to ignore, and soon they were officially together. The news spread quickly—and, understandably, Shaun and Daisy didn't take it well.

A few days later, as Charlotte and Meghan walked into work together, Meghan's tone turned cautious. "Charlotte, I need to be honest," she began gently. "Shaun's really hurt. He heard about you and Alex. He thought you two had something, and now he feels you've led him on. And Daisy—she's upset too. She feels betrayed. You know how she liked Alex, and now she thinks you crossed a line."

Charlotte stopped in her tracks, a wave of guilt washing over her. "Oh no—I never meant to hurt anyone," she said softly. "Especially not Daisy or Shaun."

Meghan nodded, sympathy flickering across her face. "I know. But it's caused tension between Shaun and Alex—they're not even speaking at the moment."

Later that day, Charlotte called Shaun to clear the air. The conversation was uneasy, every word careful, every pause weighted. She apologised sincerely for any hurt she'd caused, assuring him she'd never meant to mislead him and valued his friendship. When she hung up, guilt still lingered, but so did a quiet relief—the tension between them had eased, even if things would take time to heal.

Next, she dialled Daisy's number. "Hi, Daisy... I just wanted to say I'm really sorry," she began, her voice subdued. "I didn't mean to hurt you."

There was a long pause. When Daisy finally spoke, her voice was strained with anger. "Charlotte, you knew I liked Alex. And you still went after him. I trusted you—it feels like you crossed a line."

Charlotte's stomach knotted. "I never meant for that to happen," she said quietly. She didn't have the heart to tell Daisy that Alex had never been interested in her—that would only make things worse.

Daisy sighed, the frustration in her tone giving way to hurt. "I know you didn't, but that doesn't make it any easier."

"I understand," Charlotte murmured. "I just wanted to be honest—and to apologise. I hope we can get past this eventually."

Daisy hesitated. "I just need some time."

Charlotte exhaled, relief and shame intertwining. She had reached out, done what she could—now all she could do was wait.

She tried calling Alex but couldn't get through. Each attempt went to voicemail, and as the days passed without a reply, her worry deepened.

I guess he's changed his mind about me, Charlotte thought, staring at her phone for what felt like the hundredth time. *Maybe he thinks I just string people along.*

She replayed their last conversation in her head, searching for anything she might have said wrong. Even a simple text would have been something—some sign that he still cared. But there was nothing.

By the third evening, she had almost convinced herself it was over before it had even begun.

Then, a few days later, her phone rang unexpectedly.

"Hi, Charlotte—I'm so sorry I haven't been in touch. I went to stay with my mum for a couple of days and then came down with a bad flu. I was stuck in bed for over a week," Alex said, his voice apologetic.

"Oh no, I'm sorry to hear that. I hope you're okay. I heard about the fallout with Shaun and assumed you didn't want to see me again," she said softly.

"Don't be daft! That was tough with Shaun, but nothing's going to stop me being with you," he replied firmly.

"Except the flu, I guess," Charlotte said with a small smile.

"Ha, yes—apart from that. Anyway, can you be ready by 10 a.m. this Saturday?"

"Er... I guess so. What's happening then?" she asked, intrigued.

"I want to take you to my hometown—introduce you to my family and friends," he said, his tone warm and certain.

"Oh... right. Okay," Charlotte replied, caught off guard.

Alex chuckled. "Yeah, I want to show you off. I already

showed my friends your photo—they were very impressed."

Charlotte felt warmth spread through her. "Wow. Alright. I look forward to meeting everyone," she said, genuinely touched.

From then on, Alex chipped away at her fears with every gesture. He adored her and wrapped her in a sense of safety and love. Slowly, any insecurities she had began to fade.

For Charlotte, love had never aligned. When someone liked her, she couldn't reciprocate—and the rare times she felt strongly, her feelings went unreturned. But with Alex, it was different. Their emotions matched, and he reassured her that things wouldn't fall apart.

The road to love hadn't been straight; it had twisted through heartbreaks and hard lessons. But now, Charlotte wasn't bracing for disappointment or holding herself back in fear. For the first time, she was stepping forward with certainty—because this time, she had finally found *the one.*

MARRAKECH

CHAPTER ONE
TRAVEL APPREHENSIONS

"Don't forget—7 p.m. at mine!" Deborah called out enthusiastically as she closed her laptop and rose from her desk.

"Oh, yes!" replied Louisa, suddenly recalling her invitation for curry at Deborah's that evening.

Louisa was two years into her exciting job at a software company and had made fast friends with two like-minded colleagues, Deborah and Anne. Both were great fun to have in the office, with Anne in particular being their go-to for the latest gossip.

That evening, as Louisa pulled into the driveway of an upscale gated development, she spotted Anne stepping out of her car.

"Hey, Anne! Wait up!" she called, realising she had no clue which apartment Deborah lived in.

"I'm starving," Anne admitted as Louisa caught up to her.

"Same! I can't wait to try Deborah's curry," she replied, her stomach already grumbling in agreement.

Deborah greeted them with a wide smile, ushering them inside her new apartment and handing them drinks before they even had a chance to take off their coats. After a quick tour of her stylish space and some office gossip, the conversation swiftly shifted to their upcoming work trip.

"So, did you see Bruce's email?" Deborah asked, raising an eyebrow.

"I did… and I have to say, I'm feeling pretty nervous," Louisa admitted.

"Don't be!" Anne chimed in. "We'll all be together. There's nothing to worry about."

"Exactly," Deborah added. "You have to come, Lou!"

The email in question had come from their department manager about the forthcoming trip to Marrakech, Morocco. It was early spring 2003, just days after US and UK military forces had invaded Iraq, and concerns were growing about whether it was safe for Western travellers to visit North African or Middle Eastern countries during such a sensitive time.

"It's easy for you two to say it'll be fine—you're seasoned travellers," Louisa said. "Every time I leave the UK, something bad seems to happen."

"Like what?" Deborah smirked.

"Well, remember our team trip to Moscow last year? I got stuck at airport security while the rest of you skipped off to collect your luggage! They almost didn't let me into the country because they didn't believe I was the person in my passport photo!"

"But they did let you in, didn't they?" Anne pointed out.

"Eventually, yes—but then I had the ordeal of being accosted by four armed policemen that evening when Lars, a couple of others, and I decided to separate from the group and go for an evening stroll," Louisa recalled. "It was quite scary."

"I remember Lars saying he had to bribe the police with roubles to get them to let you go," Anne laughed. "Didn't they mistake you for... let's say, ladies of the night?"

"Something like that. But it wasn't funny—I was traumatised!" Louisa protested.

"That was one bad experience," Deborah shrugged. "It doesn't mean you'll have a bad time every time you travel."

"No?" she countered. "What about my time in Tunisia? I didn't even feel safe in my five-star hotel because the male staff wouldn't stop harassing me whenever I was alone. Or Majorca, when another tourist trapped me and a friend in their apartment? Or that time in Gare du Nord in Paris when a complete stranger touched me inappropriately?"

"Unfortunate, yes," Deborah replied, "but those things could just as easily happen in the UK. Anyhow, we'll be together in a big group this time—safety in numbers."

Deborah and Anne seemed unfazed by the government warnings, while Louisa wondered if she was being overly anxious.

"You know what... I'll come!" she exclaimed, feeling a sudden surge of determination. "Like you said, we'll be in a big group, so what could really go wrong?"

"Yay!" Deborah and Anne squealed in unison, their faces lighting up with excitement.

In the days leading up to the trip, Louisa made a conscious effort to avoid watching the news, not wanting to second-guess her decision to visit Morocco. Despite a lingering sense of unease as she packed the last of her things, she focused on the positives: they'd be staying in a luxury hotel in the heart of Marrakech, and the forecast promised glorious weather. It would be a welcome escape from the wind and rain currently battering the UK.

CHAPTER TWO
UNFAMILIAR TERRITORY

Stepping off the plane and onto the warm tarmac, Louisa felt the sun's gentle heat on her face, and a smile tugged at her lips. Her travel anxieties had mostly eased, and she was eager to check into the hotel and enjoy the evening entertainment the company had planned.

The hotel was stunning, with friendly staff greeting her and her colleagues upon arrival. After unpacking and a quick refresh, they gathered in the lobby, ready for dinner. After struggling with meals in Russia the previous year, Louisa was relieved to hear that Morocco offered exceptional cuisine, especially a wide range of vegetarian dishes.

They strolled into the hotel's courtyard, where round tables adorned with candles awaited them. It felt as though the hotel had created a special area just for their company. Instead of menus, the hotel welcomed them with a traditional Moroccan banquet, showcasing its hospitality.

As the sole vegetarian in the group, the staff served Louisa ahead of the others. While it was thoughtful to be catered for first, she felt the weight of everyone's eyes as she stared blankly at the unfamiliar food on her plate.

"That looks amazing!" Anne commented, beaming. "They really have prepared a traditional Moroccan welcome dinner for us."

Louisa smiled awkwardly, taking small bites of the only familiar item on her plate—a slice of bread. Fortunately, the rest of the group were served soon after, sparing her from further scrutiny.

Still pushing the food around her plate, a concerned waitress hurried over.

"Is everything okay with your meal?" she asked.

"Oh, yes, it's lovely. I'm just not feeling very hungry—got a bit of a headache," Louisa said, offering an excuse.

"Oh dear, shall we call a doctor?" the waitress asked, worry evident in her voice.

"No, no, I'll be fine," Louisa replied quickly, now acutely aware of the hotel staff and her colleagues' attention on her.

Thankfully, the evening's entertainment began, stealing the spotlight. Smiles and applause erupted all around as a belly dancer paraded through the courtyard and around each table, bringing much cheer as everyone sipped their wine and clapped along to the music.

As the night drew to a close, they made their way back inside the hotel. Passing through the lobby, Louisa, Deborah, and Anne noticed groups of people gathered beneath overhead TV screens, watching live news coverage of the invasion of Iraq. A hush fell over the space. British and Moroccan guests stood side by side, silently absorbing the footage—each no doubt holding different perspectives.

A sense of unease crept in as Louisa noticed the occasional look of disdain from some Moroccan guests in their direction. She could almost feel their thoughts accusing them of being complicit in the conflict. Though the war wasn't directly between the UK and Morocco, it felt as if the world was split into opposing sides: Western countries on one, and Arab countries on the other. She wanted to shout that she didn't support the war, but she kept quiet. Her colleagues seemed far less bothered.

"Wow, it's all happening," Deborah remarked, stepping away from the screen.

"Yes. This reminds me of when we were glued to the TV during nine-eleven a couple of years back," Anne added, her voice slightly sombre.

"That was such an awful day. I spent the entire afternoon thinking we were at risk, working for an American company— I kept looking out of the windows wondering if we would be targeted next," Louisa remembered.

The girls attempted to put any negative thoughts to the back of their minds as they headed upstairs to get a good night's sleep.

The next morning, after breakfast, Louisa and her colleagues ventured into Marrakech's famous souks. The bustling market was a sensory overload, with vibrant displays of spices, scarves, and an array of exotic items—including some less pleasant surprises, like dead animals hanging openly for sale. As an animal lover, Louisa found this part disturbing, but the lively atmosphere of the souks kept her intrigued.

"How much?" enquired Deborah as they stopped to admire an array of beautiful scarves. Despite the stall owner advising that the scarf was two hundred dirhams, she offered him only one hundred. Louisa was a little shocked by this.

"Pssst, Deborah, why are you offering him less money? He told you it was worth twice that!" Louisa whispered, feeling a little embarrassed that she'd tried to knock him down on price.

"See, this is why you need to travel more, Louisa—have you never heard of haggling?" laughed Deborah.

This was not something Louisa was accustomed to at all. She was used to entering a shop and paying the price listed for an item.

As Louisa observed Deborah confidently haggling back and forth with the stall owner, they eventually agreed on a price of one hundred and forty-five dirhams. Deborah handed over her cash, looking rather smug.

"See," said Deborah, smiling. "They expect you to haggle. Nobody ever pays the full price in these places."

"So, what's the point of them even putting a price on anything?" Louisa asked.

"Well, you need a starting point to work with," smiled Anne.

Louisa was torn between thinking she should travel less to avoid the stress and hassle of things like haggling—or maybe she needed to travel more to desensitise herself to it all.

The souks were overwhelming, with sellers vying for their attention at every turn, but there was a warmth and friendliness about them—albeit motivated by business.

As they wandered back, Anne turned to Louisa with a grin. "I can't believe you were so worried about coming; I told you everything would be fine."

"Yes," Louisa admitted. "The people have been friendly—though they are smiling at us while taking our money, of course."

"Well," Anne quipped, "it's still more friendly here than some places back in the UK."

"Maybe so, but have you noticed the locals?" Louisa asked. "The ones who are shopping alongside us or just going about their regular day-to-day lives? I'm sure I'm not imagining their scowls and looks of disgust as we walk among them, as they realise from our accents that we're a group of British and American tourists."

As they navigated the crowded streets, Louisa was acutely aware of not wanting to draw attention to the fact that they were Westerners. Her colleagues, however, seemed unfazed, laughing and chatting loudly as they moved through the throng of people. Their carefree attitudes contrasted sharply with Louisa's cautiousness.

CHAPTER THREE
INTO THE UNKNOWN

By the time they returned to the hotel, Louisa felt a wave of relief wash over her, grateful to escape the bustling crowds. During a quick lunch, they turned their attention to the afternoon's activity, generously arranged by the company.

"I'm really looking forward to this afternoon," Louisa said, feeling a surge of excitement. "I love a good spa day!"

"Same here," Anne responded. "Especially since it's a traditional Moroccan spa—I'm curious to see how it differs from the ones back home."

With anticipation running high, they eagerly boarded the coach, settling in for what promised to be an afternoon of relaxation. As Louisa gazed out the window, sunlight streaming through the glass, she overheard her colleagues' animated conversations filling the air around her.

In that moment, she paused to appreciate just how fortunate they were to work for a company that would fly them to another country, put them up in luxury, entertain them, and now treat them to a spa day—all while they were being paid for their time.

As the coach left the city behind, winding down quiet, unmarked roads, the chatter shifted to other travel plans.

"I can't wait to visit the south of France this summer," Anne commented.

"Lovely—which part?" Deborah inquired.

"I'm heading to the French Riviera with my mum and sister. Sometimes we visit Strasbourg, where my mum's family are from, too," Anne replied.

Deborah smiled. "Mark and I are off to Cyprus—ten days, all-inclusive."

Her mention of Cyprus stirred a memory. "That reminds me of another travel disaster," Louisa said, laughing.

"Disaster? You didn't like Cyprus? It's perfect—sun, beaches, friendly locals, great food..." Deborah looked surprised.

"Oh, I loved all of that," said Louisa. "But I twisted my ankle running away from a pushy bar promoter and spent two days laid up in bed icing it. Just when I recovered, my friend ended up in the local hospital with a bad reaction to sunscreen—not exactly the best holiday."

Anne laughed. "Unlucky, but you can't blame Cyprus for that."

"I suppose not," Louisa admitted with a smile. Glancing out the window, she added, "Oh look—we're stopping, but I don't see a spa anywhere."

Confusion spread through the group as they peered out at a plain concrete building. They seemed far from any tourist areas, on a quiet, unmarked street.

"Is this the right place? I thought we were going to a spa," Louisa asked, perplexed, as they stepped off the coach.

"It must be," Anne said, eyeing the modest entrance. "Looks like this is it."

As they got off the coach, the driver signalled for the men to use a separate entrance at the back of the building, while directing the women to the front door. They exchanged puzzled glances as they approached, wondering what lay ahead.

One of their colleagues confidently opened the door, and they filed in one by one. There was no formal reception, no friendly greeting—just the startled, disapproving stares of two naked Moroccan women, who clearly hadn't expected visitors in their private space. Awkwardly, Louisa looked away, realising they must have entered through a side or back entrance straight into the women's changing area.

The room they entered was very plain: concrete floors, white-tiled walls, and wooden benches running along the sides. It was far more basic than Louisa had imagined, but she tried to keep an open mind as she took a seat on an empty bench and began peeling off her outer layers to reveal her swimwear underneath.

Her colleagues did the same, and soon they were standing in a line, waiting for further instructions. Suddenly, the sound of raised voices caught her attention. Two women who appeared to work at the spa were talking loudly in Arabic and gesturing for them to remove their swimwear.

"What's going on?" Louisa asked, confused.

"It seems like swimwear isn't allowed in the spa," Anne suggested. "They want us to go in naked!"

They all looked at each other, puzzled. Some of their colleagues began laughing, thinking this must be part of the traditional experience, and without much hesitation, they started removing their swimwear.

Louisa froze. She couldn't believe what was happening. They had just walked off a coach and into a building, and now she was being told to strip naked? She felt completely blindsided by the situation.

"Deborah, are you okay with this?" Louisa asked, looking for reassurance.

"Not completely," she admitted, removing her swimsuit reluctantly. "But I don't want to stay out here alone in the changing room, and they won't allow us in with our swimsuits on."

"Everyone's going along with it, Louisa," Anne added. "You'll be the odd one out if you don't join in."

Before she knew it, Louisa was standing behind her now fully naked colleagues, feeling more anxious by the second. Her heart raced as she tried to make sense of the situation. Why did they need to be naked? Were the men in their group facing the same instructions next door? Was this really a spa, or was something else going on?

A flood of panicked thoughts raced through Louisa's mind. They were in the middle of nowhere; the coach had driven off, and she had no idea where she would go if she left. Fear clouded her judgment. Thoughts of the cultural tensions between the West and North Africa then resurfaced in her mind, amplifying her unease. Were they facing hostility because of who they were?

Suddenly, compliance felt like the only option, driven by fear rather than comfort. Though she wasn't at all okay with the idea of being naked in front of her colleagues, she began reluctantly removing her swimwear, dreading what might happen next.

CHAPTER FOUR
SHELL-SHOCKED

They were ushered into the next room in groups of three, leaving the majority behind, standing in line, watching and waiting. Louisa quickly noticed that all the Moroccan women in the spa, both staff and visitors, were completely naked. Perhaps this was a cultural norm?

The room they now entered was similar to the changing area and resembled a large communal shower. There were no privacy screens and certainly no signs of the plush towels or robes you would typically associate with a spa. Louisa had never felt further from home.

"I think I remember Bruce saying that it was more of a cultural cleansing experience rather than a traditional spa," whispered Anne.

Louisa watched as her colleagues sat naked on the cold, concrete floor, being scrubbed from head to toe by middle-aged, over-sized women who were also naked. They worked briskly, using metal buckets of water and stiff-bristled brushes—the kind you might use to scrub kitchen tiles.

Louisa stood there, naked, frozen, and awkward, as she watched her colleagues being scrubbed with an intensity that left them looking helpless. The staff spoke loudly to each other in Arabic, their voices echoing through the room as they continued their vigorous work.

Louisa's turn was coming. Colleague after colleague stood up after their scrub, looking shocked and bemused, before walking back to the changing area. Finally, it was

Louisa's turn. She was gestured to sit on the hard, concrete floor. She offered a nervous smile, hoping for some reassurance, but none came. She took a deep breath and braced herself.

The woman barely acknowledged Louisa. She scrubbed her body with a force that left Louisa wincing, her only communication being the occasional gesture for her to turn around. The aggressive conversations between the women continued, creating an atmosphere of disconnection, as though Louisa wasn't even there.

She was relieved to have her friends in the same room, yet equally embarrassed that they, along with strangers, were witnessing her discomfort. At times, the entire situation felt surreal, as though she were trapped in a bad dream.

No part of her body was left untouched. The stiff brush dragged across her skin, causing pain that bordered on unbearable. It felt less like a spa treatment and more like punishment. She couldn't shake the feeling that she was being punished for being an outsider—a Westerner daring to seek leisure in a place where the hurt of a distant war still lingered, shared by those who felt connected to its victims.

Eventually, the ordeal ended. Despite feeling mistreated, she mumbled a thank you before quickly heading to the changing area, eager to escape.

Outside, the coach was waiting, and Louisa boarded as quickly as she could. As she walked down the aisle to find a seat, she noticed many of her male colleagues already seated, smiling and chatting as though nothing unusual had happened. Had they experienced the same treatment? She wanted to ask but found herself speechless.

Louisa sat down near Deborah and Anne, who were laughing and chatting, their conversation entirely unrelated to the "spa" experience. All around her, others discussed dinner plans and casual topics, while Louisa felt numb. Words wouldn't come. She sat staring out of the window, silent and shell-shocked, for the entire journey back to the hotel.

What had just happened to her?

CHAPTER FIVE
BREAKING BOUNDARIES

Back in her hotel room, Louisa was still reeling from the afternoon's events. In an effort to shake off the unsettling experience, she decided to take a shower. It felt ironic to need cleansing after what was supposed to be a cleansing ritual, but she desperately wanted to distance herself from what had just happened.

As the hot water steamed around her, the calming sound of the running water and the familiar scent of the shower gel began to ease her nerves. She hung her head low, closed her eyes, and let the water run over her. Taking slow, deep breaths, she focused on the soothing sound of the water cascading down and kept repeating to herself, *I got through it.*

Suddenly, she opened her eyes and gasped. There, in the shower tray, were several small drops of blood between her feet. Panic surged through her. Oh my God, I'm bleeding! Quickly, she checked her body and discovered that the bleeding was coming from one of her nipples.

In a rush, she turned off the shower and stepped out, wrapping a towel around herself. Grabbing a tissue, she pressed it to the wound, her mind racing.

As she pressed the tissue to her skin, she felt the sting of the tiny cut left from the harsh scrubbing. Somehow, the physical pain didn't compare to the emotional discomfort that still churned inside her.

Alone with her thoughts, she pondered how this trip had magnified her sense of being out of place—a foreigner in every sense. Perhaps she wasn't like Deborah or Anne, not cut out for carefree adventures or cultural experiences. *This was a mistake—I should never have come here*, she thought.

"You alright?" Anne asked as Louisa departed the bathroom.

"Yeah… just still shocked by that so-called "spa" experience," she replied, forcing a small smile.

"Yeah, that was certainly different, wasn't it? I'm just going to find Deborah to check what time we're meeting up for dinner," Anne added with a smile as she left the room, leaving Louisa alone again with her thoughts.

She wandered through the late afternoon in a quiet haze until evening came.

As the sun set over Marrakech, Louisa rejoined her friends and colleagues. They dined at a renowned restaurant in the heart of the city, soaking in the warmth and vibrancy of the local atmosphere.

Louisa's colleagues were all in high spirits, laughing and joking as the drinks flowed.

Louisa sat back, quietly sipping her wine, watching as everyone shared their impressions of the day. No one had quite anticipated the "spa" experience they ended up with, but most shrugged it off with laughter. Their easy reactions made her pause and reflect.

Taking another sip and listening to the music playing in the background, Louisa felt a quiet resolve settling within her. She began to relax and soak in her surroundings.

The following day, they packed for their journey home. Louisa thought she'd feel relieved to leave, yet instead, she felt a little deflated. Had she really experienced the essence of Marrakech? Confusion and fear had clouded the trip, fuelled by a looming conflict. If only they'd arrived a couple of months earlier—it might have been a very different experience.

Once back at home with her parents, Louisa found herself reflecting on the trip and discussing the possibility that tensions related to Iraq's impending invasion had caused some of the unease.

"We never really know what the media tells each country during times of conflict," her mum commented. "And don't forget, political tensions can make even the safest places feel uncertain. Remember Bournemouth Pier?"

"Oh yes! That was 1993, wasn't it?" Louisa replied.

"Yes," her dad added. "We were so fortunate that there was a mechanical fault in that explosive; otherwise, that could have been the end of all of us—and the Pier. And all of that happened right here on British soil!"

"True..." she mused. "Bad things can happen anywhere. Maybe I'll return to Morocco one day, once things have calmed down. I don't want to let fear limit me—there's a whole world out there waiting to be explored."

"Maybe you could start with exploring locally," suggested Louisa's mum. "Like with the local library—I noticed six books in your room which are overdue and need returning!"

"Oh yes. I keep forgetting—I'll pop to the library this afternoon; I think they're open until 5 p.m. today," Louisa replied.

Later that day, Louisa returned her six overdue books to the library. As she was about to leave, her eye caught a new title in the Astrology section.

Astr...o...cartography? she mouthed, pulling the new book from the shelf.

By Monday, she was back in the office, practically bursting through the door, a new library book tucked under her arm.

"Deborah! Anne! You have to see this!" she exclaimed, slamming the book on the table, a loose sheet of paper fluttering out.

"It's a map," she explained, breathless. "Apparently the stars draw lines across the world—lines that show where you'll grow, work, love..."

Anne raised a brow. "And?"

Louisa grinned, tapping the page. "One of my strongest lines runs straight through North Africa. Maybe Morocco wasn't a mistake after all."

Her friends exchanged a knowing look as Louisa leaned in, eyes bright.

"So... who's ready to see where your stars lead you?" She tapped the map again, softer this time.

"I think I already know where mine are pointing—right back to Marrakech! Who's up for a quick trip to the travel agents at lunchtime?!"

ABOUT THE AUTHOR

L.J. Perkins, a UK-based author, began her writing journey after a rewarding career in IT and a family-focused career break. With a lifelong love of storytelling and music, she channels her passions into crafting evocative narratives.

After releasing her debut eBook, *An Introvert's Odyssey,* shortly followed by two additional eBooks, she brought all three together in a physical edition, *Against All Odds*, which earned five-star reviews on Amazon.

Drawing on her own life experiences, L.J. Perkins weaves personal insight with fiction—often inspired by her childhood and young adult diaries—to create stories that resonate with authenticity and heart.

With each new release, she continues to engage readers through her thoughtful storytelling and unique perspective, inviting them to explore the world through her introspective and imaginative lens.

Printed in Dunstable, United Kingdom